Books by Skoot Larson

The Lars Lindstrom Zen Jazz Mystery series:

The No News is Bad News Blues

The Real Gone Horn Gone Blues

The Dig You Later Alligator Blues

The On the Road Again Blues

The Dave Holman "Texas" Mystery series:

Copkiller

The Texas Detective

The Pachyderm Predicament

The Ivory Coast Puzzle

Political Humor

Apollo Issue, a Humorous Look at Healthcare

The Palestine Solution

The Testament of Jessica Crystal

Fantasy

King Irv's Big Adventure

King Irv's Cabernet Caper

King Irv and the Holy Grail

Johnny's So Long at the Fair

a Dave Holman Mystery

by

Skoot Larson

Skoot's
Jazz
Books

First printing

All characters in this book are fictitious, and any resemblance to real persons, living or dead, is coincidental. Some of the locations have been renamed out of respect for the local area's history. While everything in the tale is fictional, I don't wish to defame the brave pioneers who settled the Rockport area, so places have been renamed to prevent any insults to the families that settle this community.

ISBN: 978-0-692-06768-0

Published by Skoot's Jazz Books

Rockport, Texas

For the Rockport Police, the sheriff's deputies of Aransas County, Texas, and all the other first responders who saved lives and helped our community get through Hurricane Harvey. Your efforts are deeply appreciated.

Also, thanks again to Theresa Feeser for helping put my thoughts in order so my story makes sense.

CHAPTER ONE

"**I** don't like crowds!" I told her. "Period, end of argument, nothing more to say." I fidgeted nervously with the tails of my bright Hawaiian shirt that concealed my cell phone and my old Walther PP automatic pistol.

"Oh, come on Dave," Yolanda purred. "You don't have to go out and mingle with all these people. Just hand them a brochure when they stop here at our booth. Ask them to put a few bucks in the jar to help save these beautiful animals."

My part-time assistant and full time special lady, Yolanda, had dragged me to the Rockport Sea Fair, an annual fundraiser for our small beachside community's Chamber of Commerce. She had paid a few hundred dollars for a booth to advertise that she rescues elephants, both Indian and African, although all the pachyderms she had saved to date were as Indian as she herself pretended to be.

The fair was set up on a triangular patch of pasture bordered by Rockport Beach on the south end, Little Bay to the north-east and Texas Highway 35 Business on the other leg.

Yolanda had acquired the booth to advertise her charity organization, the "Rockport Elephant Rescue." The powers-that-be had placed us just across a narrow grassy aisle from the stage end of the entertainment tent, subjecting us to loud country rock music, while on our other side, a collection of carnival thrill rides filled what was normally a parking lot for Rockport Beach. One ear was filled with twangy guitar and bad singing while the other echoed with squeals of fright and delight.

I checked the left rear pocket of my shorts once again to be sure I had my hip flask of single malt Scotch on my person. It was going to be a long weekend.

To draw attention to herself and her charitable organization, Yolanda was dressed in her ethnic saffron sari. She was barefoot and had placed a red dot on her forehead, where spiritual types might claim she had her 'third eye.' I often joked with the guys at Rusty's Tropical Grill and Bar that if they rubbed the dot off her forehead, they might win a 7-11 store.

"So can I trust you here for a few minutes while I scout around the fair?" Yolanda smiled down on me like a mother scolding a small child.

"Yeah, I'll be alright," I told her. "Can you bring me back a beer while you're out?"

"I thought you didn't drink cheap commercial beer." She gave me an amused look over the top of her sunglasses. "I don't think they have anything but Budweiser and Miller Light here."

"Well," I drawled, "I saw someone with a large, maybe 16 ounce can. I think it was some kind of Mexican lager… Montejo, I think it was."

She laughed. "That's my Dave, quantity over quality in a pinch!"

I looked away. "Yeah, well, it looks like it's going to be a hot afternoon."

Yolanda shook her head, turned her back to me and walked off with her cute little body swaying in her yellow robes.

Waiting for Yolanda to return with my beer, I amused myself by watching the babes that strolled by, except these young girls all looked a bit weird for my taste. They had tattoos, piercings, and a few had beer guts that would make an old cowboy proud. This wasn't the kind of world I grew up in!

My eyes drifted to the carnival rides on the shore of Rockport Beach. There was a pair of those hammer things that spin folks upside down while flying an ellipse through the air. There was a tilt-a-whirl, spinning tea cups a la Disneyland's Alice in Wonderland, and an enormous Ferris wheel rising above the rest of the rides and over-priced carnival food wagons.

My eyes were drawn to one of the gondolas half-way up that giant vertical wheel. As the car rocked wildly, there seemed to be two people struggling together. The way they were turned to face one another, I wondered about the safety harnesses they were supposed to be belted into. It was almost as though they were trying to wrestle on that tiny bench a hundred feet in the air. I couldn't take my eyes off this scene.

Just as their gondola reached the pinnacle of the ride's height, one of the figures stood up grasping the other, lifting him from the bench and twisting sidewise. The captive figure let out a terrified scream of "Nooooo" just before he was launched over the side.

The young man plummeted straight down. I watched in horror as the body fell directly into the gears and motor below that were turning the giant ride. I glanced at my watch and noted the time; one-forty-three in the afternoon, October 14, 2017.

No one else seemed to notice for the longest time, until the man operating the giant wheel turned to see blood spurting from the power source of his big wheel. All at once, screams rose from the crowd as fingers pointed and other folks on the ride shouted in panic.

CHAPTER TWO

I felt trapped! Yolanda was out strolling around the fairgrounds while I was watching a crime in progress! Did I dare leave my post at her booth? Could I live with myself if I didn't? And could I live with my partner if I did?

I paced restlessly back and forth across the ten by ten square behind a card table filled with brochures, a large donation jar and a clay statue of an Indian elephant. I glanced behind me at the canvas divider covered with travel posters for India and Sri Lanka, each poster featuring a magnificent gray pachyderm front and center. I willed Yolanda to return as I watched city and country trucks arrive with bright scarlet and blue lights flashing from their roofs.

It was probably only a matter of minutes that seemed like hour before I saw a smiling Yolanda approaching, a large can of beer in one hand and a tray of something that looked like Vietnamese food in the other. There was no time for explanations.

"Thanks," I shouted, as I sprinted over her display table towards the carnival area. "Be back as soon as I can. I don't mind if the beer gets warm!"

Her face registered surprise, then she shook her head and shot me a quick smile when she noticed all the emergency vehicles arriving just beyond our little booth.

I got to the base of the tall Ferris wheel just as the uniforms were spreading crime scene tape around the ride. An officer I recognized but couldn't put a name to had the boy who'd thrown his partner from the ride seated in the back of a Rockport Police SUV and appeared to be interrogating him. I didn't know the officer who was taking charge, but when I told him my name he nodded to his team that I should be permitted inside the cordoned off area.

"Okay, Holman," he said with a serious face. "I've heard you tend to show up when things like this happen, so what's the story?"

"I just happened to be looking at the Ferris wheel when someone pushed our victim out of his car," I relayed breathlessly, nodding toward the lad seated in the police vehicle.

"Pushed?" the officer repeated. "That's a strong statement, Holman. Pushed? Are you sure of that?"

"Hey, I saw two people wrestling on the ride. It looked like they'd undone their safety harnesses. One figure twisted the other one around and it looked like he threw him over the side of the gondola."

"Well, Holman, that's quite a story... But we've just taken the very upset young man from the gondola of the ride in question. He's the son of one of Rockport's most prominent attorneys and the county's wealthiest property owners. The young man tells us that his friend was high on something and undid his safety harness. The victim told our young witness that he thought he could fly. This young man we're talking with tells us he tried to hold his friend down, but the young man broke free of his grasp and leaped over the side. The young man, AJ Laudermaelk, was trying to save the other boy. That was probably the struggle you think you saw."

"That's not the way it looked from where I was watching…"

"Holman, we'll be glad to take a statement from you Monday morning, but I don't think it will be necessary. The young man in question is AJ Laudermaelk the fourth. You know the family! If young AJ says that's what happened, we must be inclined to believe it."

"Just because someone is from one of the oldest families in the area you won't question his story?"

"Come on. Holman, you know how it works here in Texas."

"No, sir… What was your name?"

"I don't have to give you a name, Holman!"

"Well, it will be easy enough to check the duty roster when I come in on Monday, and, no, I don't accept how it works in Texas. I spent twenty-two years working the worst neighborhoods of Los Angeles, California, and I'm suspicious of anyone hiding behind a family name."

"This interview is over," the officer said with a frown. "Can someone escort Mr. Holman outside the crime scene please? And make sure he doesn't try to come back in!"

CHAPTER THREE

B ack at our Elephant Rescue booth, I finished the large Mexican beer Yolanda had brought in about two swallows. I didn't have any appetite for the egg rolls and shrimp. I wasn't quite sure what was going on here, but something didn't feel right. I asked Yolanda where I could get another beer. It might help me get my head together. I'd save the scotch in my hip flask for later, when things really got weird! It looked like it would be a long day; maybe a long weekend.

Rockport homicide detective, Loretta Sanchez, rode by in an official Sea Fair golf cart. I bolted from Yolanda's booth and chased her down. Lola was in uniform, volunteering for some civic duty to help out the Sea Fair charities.

I jumped onto the running board of the small plastic vehicle, asking Lola Sanchez if we could talk. "Dave," she replied. "Do you know our Aransas County Constable? This is Doc Thomas, Doc, Dave Holman. Dave's a local private eye!"

Doc Thomas gave me a smile. "I didn't know we had such an animal here."

"Nice to meet you, Doc… So Lola, can we take a break and get a beer or something?"

"Dave, you know I'm on duty here." She gave me a sly wink.

"Just drop me by the main gate," Constable Doc told her. "I didn't hear a thing!"

"So what's this about?" Lola Sanchez asked when we were seated under the big top, toward the rear and away from the stage. I had bought us each a beer and found us a table some distance from anyone who might want to overhear us.

"You heard about the kid who got killed on the Ferris wheel?" I asked.

"Yeah, some kid fell to his death," she answered, giving me a hooded look. "What about it?"

"He didn't fall!" I told her forcefully. "He was pushed! I saw the whole thing."

"Oh, come on, Dave. We've got a whole crime scene team on this already. They all say the boy, some local kid named Johnny Dominguez, fell. They're ready to rule it death by misadventure."

"Lola, I watched the whole thing from Yolanda's Elephant booth, right over there. That kid was *pushed*! Thrown, actually. He was wrestling with another kid in that car and the other boy grabbed him and threw him over the side!"

Detective Loretta Sanchez drew her head back and gave me a critical up and down. "Dave, we've talked to the *other* boy that was sharing the ride. He's very distraught about his friend taking off his seat restraint and climbing out of the gondola. He swears he was trying to pull his friend back *into* the car. Maybe his struggle to save his friend *appeared* to be something else from where you were standing?"

"Lola, I know what I saw! The young man wasn't trying to hold someone in the car, he was twisting his friend over the side and pushing with all his might!"

"That can't be right Dave. Do you know who that young man is? AJ, the fourth! He's the son of Ames Jordan Laudermaelk, the third. The first Ames Jordan Laudermaelk was the son of Amy Jordan, the woman Jordan Beach was named for. The family built the Jordan Mansion back before Texas was even a republic! They're, like, the first family in this entire area of Texas!"

"And that means the boy could have done no wrong? Or does it mean that no one is brave enough to question what really happened?"

"I don't like where this conversation is going, Dave Holman! You're pretty much a newcomer here. You've been in Rockport, what, five years? I don't think you know enough about how things work in this county!" Yolanda looked at me as though I was a couple chinchillas short of a fur farm.

"Lo, I've worked small towns and big cities. Things are pretty much the same wherever you go. Money protects its own. People with big names and reputations require an even closer look than simple stick ups or domestic arguments. When there are moneyed interests involved, it's more important than ever to cross every 't' and dot every 'i'. And this kid who died, Johnny Dominguez? Doesn't he deserve a full investigation?"

"You're way too cynical, Dave! This is Rockport. Everyone knows everyone else. If you have complaints about how we are handling this, take it up with the chief or the county sheriff. Just, please, don't involve me in any of it! I *like* my job here."

CHAPTER FOUR

Down at the police station Monday morning, I was informed by the desk sergeant that Saturday's death had been ruled an accident, a "death by misadventure," I was told.

"That's so much nicer than accusing the dead boy of being high on drugs or suicidal, which we've been led to believe he was. We're thinking of his family here, Holman."

He also informed me that both Detective Sanchez and the Chief were "too busy" to see anyone this morning.

"The investigating officers believe that the deceased young man, ah, Johnny Dominguez I believe his name was, had wiggled out of his safety harness. His friend AJ tried hard to hold onto him and save him, but young Johnny must have been pretty determined to take his own life."

"So are we talking accident or suicide here?" I asked him.

"Come on, Dave," he tsked. "Suicide is such an *ugly* word and puts a lot of bad feelings on the boy's family. Do we really want to leave that kinda stigma on those good folks?"

I started to ask for more information, but the phone on the man's desk rang. As he answered the ringing instrument, he turned his back on me. Obviously, our interview was being terminated.

Back out in my car, I tried Lola Sanchez's cell number, but it went quickly to voice mail. I silently cursed the modern technology that displayed a caller's phone number, allowing them to choose whether or not they cared to answer.

As I was putting the key in my Saab's ignition, I noticed one of the patrolman from Saturday's incident pulling into the parking lot. Had they mentioned me at that morning's roll call? It was worth a shot to approach the officer with a question or two. Worst case scenario was that he, too, might ignore me.

As it turned out, Officer Lon Kravitz hadn't been warned against speaking to me.

"We were under a lot of pressure out there," he told me. "The carnie people had to get to McAllen by Tuesday afternoon for another event and they had some big time attorney threatening to sue the city if they missed their gig. We knew it wasn't their fault, I mean the last thing those people wanted was some kid getting killed on one of their rides, f'christ sake!"

"Do carnivals usually have a powerful attorney on retainer?" I asked. "I mean, I always thought those folks operated on a shoe string budget."

"Well, I don't think they had this guy on a retainer or anything. He was a local guy who stepped up to help them out."

"A local guy?"

"Yeah, a guy who lives local, or at least he has a home near here on Copano Bay. I think his law office is up in Austin, but he has a small satellite office here near the county courthouse."

"Does this guy have a name?"

"Yeah, Ames Laudermaelk. He's the heir to the Jordan estate up in Jordan Beach."

"Wasn't it his kid who was up on that Ferris wheel with the vic...?"

"I don't know anything about *that*, but I'm sure it's just a coincidence." Kravitz glanced nervously toward the police station's back door. "Anyway, I got work to do, Holman. See you up at Rusty's some time."

I was beginning to smell rats at every bend in the highway. Big rats with big red eyes! Living here in Rockport for just over five years, I had found it to be an honest and upstanding community. I'd discovered corruption in neighboring communities like Port Aransas and Corpus Christi, and I'd done my best to put a stop to the wrong I found there.

Now something wicked was rearing its head much closer to home, too close for my liking, and I had no excuse to get involved without bringing trouble on myself.

I drove past my Market Street office, taking a brief detour by the Bottle Brothel Liquor Emporium for an overpriced bottle of good whiskey, before returning. I wisely surmised that the depression coming over me was more than a cheap bottle of booze could handle, so I sprung for some Jameson's.

An Irish whiskey buzz would lighten my load today. If I felt better tomorrow and the autumn temperature was over seventy-two degrees, I'd take a long meditative walk along Rockport Beach.

Betsy, the Bottle Brothel's proprietor, was occupying her rocking chair on the front porch, as usual.

"Mornin', Holman. You're up and running early today."

"Just showing my support for local business," I told her, wearing a false smile I didn't feel.

"Dave, you can't shit a shitter," Betsy retorted, turning a gap-toothed grin my way. "I know you prefer scotch to bourbon, Dave, but ask one of the girls to loan you a coffee cup from the back room. Let me pour you a finger or two of what I'm drinkin' and tell me what's got you down."

CHAPTER FIVE

Settling down, I explained to Betsy, the redneck psychologist, how I'd been helping Yolanda with her elephant booth at Sea Fair. Betsy gave me a funny look at the mention of my partner. They didn't like each other, and probably never would.

Although Betsy and I weren't really close, she always said that Yolanda wasn't good enough for me. Yolanda didn't like Betsy because she thought marketing booze by employing scantily clad ladies as clerks was demeaning to women, all women, never mind that Betsy paid her girls better than the help at any other place serving booze in Aransas County, package store or saloon.

When I got to the part about the young man falling from the ride, Betsy nodded and told me, "I read about that."

When I mentioned that AJ the fourth had been the boy in the car with Johnny, Betsy gave a knowing nod and put a finger beside her nose. "Yeah, that would be right," she told me. "That whole family has always been rotten, rotten to the core!"

Ariel, from the front counter of the Bottle Brothel, emerged through the front door and handed me a chipped souvenir Port Aransas mug, which Betsy promptly half-filled with bourbon from a jug nestled in her shawl.

"What do you mean, always been rotten?" I asked before taking a small sip of the brown liquid.

"If you've got a few minutes, Holman, I'll give you a short history lesson of this area."

She turned her eyes to mine and I dipped my head that it would be alright.

"This goes way back, almost to the time when Aransas County split off from Refugio County. You know the Jordan Mansion, up there on its namesake beach?"

"I've seen the historic marker signs," I told her, "but I never stopped to check it out."

"Well maybe you should, Holman. It's quite a piece of early Texas architecture. Anyway, just after the first decade of the last century, old Milburn Jordan took him a young wife, a headstrong woman who immediately took over the family business dealings. Milburn never showed much aptitude for running the ranch."

Betsy looked into my eyes and knew she had me hooked, so she continued.

"Ol' Milburn, he was a scrapper. Always picking fights with his neighbors and trying to figure ways to steal their land and their livestock. It was no surprise when he turned up floatin' in Copano Bay with a bullet hole in his head."

"He was murdered?" I asked.

"That idea was seriously kicked around," Betsy told me, "but the sheriff at the time didn't look into it too hard. It was rumored that Milburn's young wife, Amy, and the sheriff had a fondness for each other. Milburn Jordan wasn't a real popular man around here anyway.

"And Amy Jordan was just in a hurry to get everything settled so she could take control of the family fortune."

"Ah, the old Wild West," I sighed, taking another sip of the lady's whiskey.

Betsy gave me an odd, sideways look, then continued.

"At the start of the Depression, an aimless drifter who called himself Johannes Laudermaelk passed through on a Texas and New Orleans freight train. Johannes stopped for a day or two, looking to maybe settle on the Texas coast. He tried his hand at odd jobs and soon became the handyman for Amy Jordan's place. All the locals were suspicious of this guy, but Amy Jordan had chosen him, so he was accepted.

"Amy and Johannes were married the next year, just before she had a baby, a son they called Ames Jordan Laudermaelk."

"Interesting stuff," I told Betsy, holding my cup out for more whiskey. Her story, along with a mild buzz, was starting to take my mind off the troubles of the Sea Fair incident.

"The first Ames Jordan Laudermaelk volunteered at the start of World War II. He was soon dishonorably discharged from the army. It was very hushed up, but rumor has it he was molesting young boys near his duty station in Berlin right after the war."

Now I was really getting drawn in to Betsy's tale.

"For each generation, there has only been one son carrying on the Jordan/Laudermaelk name." She turned to give me a wink and a grin. "If they didn't own almost half the county, someone might give voice to what we all have suspected for sixty-some years. This entire Jordan clan are a bunch of child molesters! I think that's why

Jordan the Third spends more time in Austin than here at home in Aransas County!"

"Any solid proof?" I asked my friend.

"When you're rich enough to buy off anyone who might complain," Betsy told me with a smirk, "it's tough to get a serious complaint. The last family who tried to stand up to AJ the third died in a boating accident, 1972 was the year, I believe. The Coast Guard said they had tried to take a shortcut into the bay over a shallow oyster bank, tearing the hull from under their boat. Their son, who claimed AJ had force him to commit unnatural acts, was in the wrecked boat with his parents and two sisters when they pulled the broken hull off the rocks. The entire family, it was reported, were below decks at the time and didn't have a chance to escape.

"So who was on the bridge guiding the boat out of Jordan Harbor?"

"Quite a few folks asked that question, but no one ever got a straight answer," Betsy told me.

CHAPTER SIX

etsy's story played on my mind for the rest of the day and night. I decided to get on my bicycle and peddle up the coast to check out the Jordan Mansion. It was a tall narrow structure, two stories high with some sort of cupola above the second floor. The was raised on a high foundation, probably to protect against the storm surge that might accompany a hurricane or other heavy weather.

I walked around the grounds to check it from all angles and found a small visitor center on the street behind the mansion. A dark-haired twenty-something with a wide, perfect smile asked if I was visiting from out of town. When I told her I was a Rockport resident, she asked if I would be so kind as to sign their guest register, which I did.

Beyond her desk and a small gift shop, there were display cases with Jordan family artifacts that dated back to the mansion's construction; a china dinner service, Amy Jordan's wedding dress, some hand-made furniture and things like that. There were also five-foot high poster-board cut outs of some of the Jordan and Laudermaelk family members blown up from old photographs. From what I was seeing, the most attractive thing about Amy Jordan must have been her money. Johannes Laudermaelk looked like a reject from a Haight-Ashbury commune of the 1960s, but that was a different time and I shouldn't have expected them to look like the television cowboys I'd grown up watching. I was sure that living in nineteenth century Texas was a hard existence.

As I approached the exit, the last cutout was the current Ames Laudermaelk, wearing a western-cut suit with a cowboy hat and string tie and holding a placard thanking me for stopping by, and an advertisement for his law firm which was sponsoring current renovations of the property.

From the Jordan Mansion, I peddled a few blocks north to Rusty's to lubricate my dry throat. It was mid afternoon so the place wasn't too crowded. There were two couples from Minnesota seated at the bar sharing travel stories and a small family having lunch at one of the tables. Rusty was at the back end of the bar studying a new Louisiana cook book. I grabbed a stool close to Rusty, and Brenda brought me a Redfish Ale.

I watched a soccer match, Real Madrid playing some Italian team, for a few minutes until Rusty looked up from his studying. "You ever go over and look at the Jordan Mansion?" I asked.

"I drive by it every day," came the man's reply. "I never stopped for a closer look."

"They must've built'm pretty good back then," I offered, "considering that it's still in pretty good shape when so many modern houses are falling apart."

Rusty kind of grunted agreement and went back to reading his cook book. Without looking up, he reached for his bottle of Coors Light, tilted it to his face and discovered that the bottle was empty. "Brenda," he called out, "Could you bring me another Coors Light, dressed with a lime?" When he looked up again, anticipating his fresh beer, I asked, "Have you ever met Ames Laudermaelk?"

"Not that I know of," Rusty told me with an inquisitive face. "Why are you suddenly interested in Ames Laudermaelk?"

"I'm doing an investigation of his son," I told the man. "I suspect the kid, AJ is it, of murder."

"Whoa, tread lightly there, my friend," Rusty replied. "You're messin' with a real political super-power in old Ames. He could end up eating you for lunch. I've heard that he kinda hand- picked most the judges and top law enforcement people in this county."

"But aren't those mostly elected offices?" I asked.

"Sure they're elected," he chuckled, "Welcome to conservative south Texas. Have you had the opportunity to vote here yet?"

"I just voted in the county elections back in June," I assured my friend.

"So did you happen to notice that most of the local offices had one Republican running, unopposed?"

I had to think about that one. Sure enough, as I recalled my ballot, Rusty was right. I guess I hadn't connected the dots. Suddenly a lot of things I'd been discovering made perfect sense. If the top brass of the county were Laudermaelk's men, they wouldn't be in too big a hurry to arrest his kid. I thanked Rusty, finished my beer and called Brenda for my tab.

"You're only having one beer today, Holman?" Rusty inquired. "Are you sick or something?"

"I just remembered an important appointment," I told him. "Anyway, I'd just come up this way to look at the Jordan Mansion."

CHAPTER SEVEN

The more dead ends I encountered in asking about AJ Laudermaelk, the more curious I became and the fewer answers I seemed able to find. I was on the verge of making it a personal matter, something I'd follow up on my own, client or no client, when a distraught couple showed up on my doorstep Tuesday morning.

"Mr. Holman?" the washed-out blond woman asked.

"That's me, please come in," I replied.

She appeared to be in her late forties, but I had trouble guessing ages here in Texas. Life in this climate tended to age some people faster than others. The lady had thin legs and arms, but a protruding gut under withered breasts. Her husband was dark and rail thin with a leathery hide, as though he'd spent too many hours working outside in the sun. They both wore worn and faded blue jeans over distressed brown boots and checkered shirts with white pearl buttons.

I ushered them to the plastic patio chairs across from my desk and offered them some of Yolanda's strong coffee. The gentleman said, "Yes, please, black." His lady just wrung her hands and shook her head.

"We're the Dominguez family," the woman told me in a whiney, nasal voice.

"Our son, Johnny, died at the Sea Fair carnival," the man added. His words were half choked and seemed to stick in his throat. "We don't believe it was an accident. That AJ boy has been a sort of thorn in our son's side for as long as I can remember. Always bullying him, never gave him a minute of peace."

"So many times our Johnny came home with a bloody nose or worse," the lady put in. "He didn't want to say what happened, but we always heard from his friends that AJ had beaten him up and called him a momma's boy or queer bait or some other nasty things."

"He usually called him a dirty Mexican," Mr. Dominguez emphasized with hooded eyes and a sour face.

"I was there at Sea Fair," I told them. "I saw the whole thing and I would tend to agree with you that it wasn't an accident. I tried to report what I'd seen to the police, but no one was interested."

"So can you help us to get some justice for our Johnny?" the woman asked, almost on the verge of tears.

"First," I told them, "Can I know who I'm speaking with? I know your son was Johnny Dominguez, but what are your names?"

The woman finally let a small smile play on her lips. "I'm Melba and this is my husband, Jessie. Jessie came to this country as a small boy in the '50s. He worked in the fields alongside his parents for many years but went to school at night. Jessie got a degree in Business Administration from Southwestern College, although no one in power wants to acknowledge that fact. We've built a small but successful business here."

"I'm a labor contractor," Jesse Dominguez announced proudly. "I find laborers for my client companies, take a small percentage as a fee, and make sure that the people I contract out are paid appropriately and treated fairly. My people are bonded and their backgrounds checked so my clients know they can be trusted to do the job and do it right."

"That's a good service," I told him. "It keeps everything fair."

"But a lot of people here are not happy about what we do," Melba put in. "They want slave labor for slave wages, people they can pick up on a street corner with no questions asked and no records kept. They say they don't want to pay a 'middle-man.'"

"Greed," I said, almost without thinking. "Greed is at the heart of all this."

"Yes, exactly," Jesse said, with a faraway look in his eye. "That is what has kept my people down for hundreds of years. That is the root of slavery everywhere, greed." His wife nodded agreement.

"So you are a businessman," I gave him, "and obviously a successful one. But the local people in power won't recognize this?"

"Mr. Holman," Melba sighed with an empty laugh, "you're not from around here. I don't know how it is in California, but here in Texas they're still fighting the Battle of San Jacinto…"

"And the Civil War," her husband interjected. "A lot of these people would like to see anyone with darker skin go away; Mexicans, blacks… even Italians and Jews to hear them talk. And I've heard them at many town hall meetings and gatherings. They give me arrogant looks when they speak about the Texas they would like to see."

I had no answer to this. I almost felt guilty for being a white American of Norwegian heritage even though I had, myself, always been color-blind as far as racism was concerned.

In World War II, when my father had been sent from Minnesota to New Orleans as a young Navy lieutenant, my mother had refused to sit in front of the 'colored' sign on the street car, which caused the driver to sit for some thirty minutes before he came back and threw the 'colored' sign into the car's rear window, called my mother a rude name, and continued on their journey across town.

I had never been able to understand racism, but then I'd had the good fortune to grow up in Los Angeles, probably America's number two melting pot after New York. My friends in my youth came from all over the United States, as well as south of the border and the lands across the Pacific Ocean. In my twenty some years with the Los Angeles Police Department, my co-workers had been of a similar mix. Not so much in the early days, but increasingly over the years, as federal mandates rearranged the structure of our department.

"As an investigator, I'm supposed to be neutral about things," I told them. "But I do not tolerate discrimination or racism in any form. I was unaware of this background information when I witnessed your son being thrown from the Ferris wheel at Sea Fair. What you've told me make it even more imperative that we pursue this matter.

"I'm not that up on local politics, being from California, but fairness and justice should know no boundaries. From what you've told me, I will take your case and I won't ask for a retainer up front."

"Please, Mr. Holman," Jesse protested, "We can pay you, we want to pay you."

"I didn't say I won't take your money, I simply said that I won't ask for a retainer. I will ask for five hundred a day plus expenses when everything is settled to your satisfaction, but I will also be filing a discrimination law suit on your son's behalf. Whatever I might collect from any such suit I'll put towards your bill. And, at the same time, I'll be seeking to end the state's discrimination against you and other Hispanic businesses like yours. Called me a quixotic crusader, but I want to see this world a fairer and more right place."

Melba Dominguez started to protest but I cut her off. "I'm retired from the Los Angeles Police Department," I told her. "My pension is enough that I can afford to fight for what I believe is right. Also, I believe this is a strong enough case that I will be rewarded sufficiently for my time and effort."

Jesse Dominguez extended a hand over the table to me. "Thank you, Mr. Holman, thank you."

Melba Dominguez pushed her way past her husband around the table and threw her arms around me in a big hug.

CHAPTER EIGHT

It was tough talk with the Dominguez's, but in reality, I didn't have a clue where to start. I knew what I'd seen at Sea Fair, but half the town of Rockport didn't want to believe me, or, more likely, was afraid to admit that what I'd seen might have some base in fact. Ames Laudermaelk was a larger than life character locally. He was used to getting what he wanted and few people, politicians and law enforcement included, were willing to risk getting in his way. The word on the street was that careers could be made or broken based on a word from Ames Laudermaelk. Contacts at the local cop shop, who wouldn't look me in the eye, implied that mine could be one of those careers. It was almost as bad as when I'd first arrived here from Los Angeles.

Even Yolanda, who was always rock-steady and unshakable, seemed nervous when Ames Laudermaelk and his reputation were mentioned. She told me she didn't wish to talk about it.

I decided to start at Rockport Jordan High School. When school let out at 3:30, I parked across Enterprise Boulevard from the campus and started questioning students as they got in their cars to leave school for the day. The ROTC squad was practicing a manual-of-arms drill on one side of the parking area while other students came out in groups of two and three to make their way home.

When I mentioned AJ the fourth, many of the students hurried away or gave me a wide birth. Most of the student body was afraid to talk about their classmate. It was only a matter of minutes before a white pick-up truck with Rockport Jordan Campus Police stenciled on the doors, pulled up next to my Saab, blocking me in.

An older officer I didn't know with thick salt-and-pepper hair took his time getting out of the vehicle and coming around to my door.

"Dave Holman?" he asked politely. "I'll need you to move on from here. I've had a complaint about you harassing our students."

"I was just asking some questions..." I began, but was quickly cut off.

"I have the authority from our police chief to arrest you right here and now. We here in Rockport are dedicated to protecting our students from sexual predators and drug dealers," the man told me with a serious face. "Knowing your background here in Rockport, I don't want to do it, but you leave me no choice."

"What have I done wrong?" I inquired. "You know I'm not a sexual predator or a drug dealer. Only two years ago I rescued a handful of local girls who had been kidnapped and held as sex slaves." In answer to my protest, the man reached behind his back to bring forth handcuffs from his belt.

"Either move along or step out of the car and spread'm across your hood," he told me with a mischievous wink. "I don't want to book you, Holman but, like I said, you leave me no choice."

I started my engine, gave a small, two-fingered Boy Scout salute and put the Saab in gear. "I'll see you later up at Rusty's," the officer said in a soft voice as he backed up to give me room to drive away from the curb. As I pulled out, I caught a smile and a wink from the school policeman.

CHAPTER NINE

From the high school, I drove up to Rusty's for a beer and some contemplation. Brenda was waiting tables and filling in as part-time bartender while Rusty met with his accountant in the office.

The lady brought me a Redfish IPA and a bowl of peanuts, then went off to check on a table of late lunch diners. When she returned, Brenda offered a hug, then backed up and told me I looked a bit troubled.

"It's this Sea Fair thing," I confided. "I saw AJ the Fourth push Johnny Dominguez off that Ferris wheel, but no one wants to acknowledge that it happened. If only I could talk to the kid, ask him some questions."

"Why not go knock on his door?" Brenda asked me.

"Oh sure," I frowned into my pint glass, "Like someone is going to tell me where to find this AJ kid."

"Why not try his home?" Brenda smiled.

"What, like Ames Laudermaelk's home address is listed in the telephone book?"

Brenda laughed. "Oh right," she chuckled, "You're not from around here."

"What's that supposed to mean?" I queried.

Brenda laughed again. "Everyone knows that Ames Laudermaelk lives in a castle out on Copano Bay, at least that's his local Rockport home. He claims it's a replica of the Laudermaelk family's ancestral home in Germany, although he's never specified just *where* in Germany. That's just another facet of the jerk's whole 'better-than-thou' white-man' attitude."

I was dumbfounded. Of course with an ego as large as Ames Laudermaelk's he would brag about everything in his life. And here I had been thinking that he would keep his family secreted close to the old Jordan Mansion on the coastline.

"You might want to talk to the local JP as well," Brenda told me.

"JP?" I asked, "What's a JP?"

"Justice of the Peace," she giggled. "They preside over juvenile court, so they know all about whose naughty and nice, to borrow a phrase. I don't know how much the JP's office might be willing to share, but I would guess they aren't quite as politically connected as the cops, so they might talk to you."

"So this JP person is another lawyer, like a judge?"

Brenda laughed again. "Welcome to Texas, Dave. A Justice of the Peace down here is an *elected* official. He or she doesn't have to know the law, in reality they don't have to know much of anything. They just have to know a lot of people who'll vote for them."

"I always thought a Justice of the Peace just married people."

"Yeah," she grinned. "They can conduct weddings but they also hold small claims court and some other duties to take the load off the regular judges. They wield a lot of power in this county."

This was something to think about. I made a note to myself to look up the JP from Laudermaelk's district and have a talk with this person. I finished my ale, tipped Brenda about twice what I normally would have, and headed the old Saab west out Texas Farm to Market Road 3036. I made the twists and turns Brenda had described to me until I found Old Salt Lake Road.

The road dead-ended at a body of water that my map identified as Salt Lake. Just to the left at the end of the road was a long driveway following the shoreline. From where I sat at the intersection, I could see a Neo-Gothic fortress-like structure rising against the swampy backdrop. The building was massive, with towers rising to crenellated turrets and battlements dominating both north and south ends. It appeared to be constructed of large, gray stones fitted to form a solid wall.

Pulling up closer, I could hear a weird childlike cry; Peacocks? Here in south Texas? At the next slight bend in the driveway, one of the large green, blue and gold birds crossed the pavement in front of me. I drove on to a small parking area across a narrow channel from the faux German castle. I parked the Saab next to a wooden bridge over a dirty, green slime-choked waterway, got out of my car and headed for what I assumed to be the front door. Crossing the foot bridge to the portal, I noticed a half-dozen alligators lounging in the shallow water beneath the planks that made up the bridge.

When I pulled the chord beside the front door and heard chimes from deep within, I almost expected Ted Cassidy, "Lurch" from the Adam's family, to open the door. Instead, I heard the yapping of small dogs quickly approaching the other side of the oak door. It was opened by a very thin and disheveled bottle-blond woman who looked to be about my own age. She was dressed in a soiled party dress and clutched a martini glass in one hand; her eyes were very red. I assumed that she had started happy hour a little before I had. Two small, black dogs with faces like bats bounced and barked around her heels.

The woman looked me up and down then shot me a grin. "My, you're a tall one, aren't you? Come in, can I offer you a drink?"

"And you would be Mrs. Ames Laudermaelk?" I asked.

"You were expecting Cinderella 'cause I live in this shitty castle?" she countered. "So come in already. Name your poison."

"Well, Mrs. Laudermaelk, I'm actually looking to speak to your son, AJ. Is he at home?"

"So you prefer young boys to old broads?" she took a step back, looked me over head to toe once more and commented, "Just like my worthless husband!"

"Mrs. Laudermaelk," I began again. "I want to speak to your son regarding a legal matter. My name is Dave Holman and I'm a private investigator, so I'll ask again, is young AJ at home?"

"Dave Holman, meet Truth and Beauty." She gave me a sly wink. "They're schipperkes and they're my best friends… what the fuck, they're my only friends." For a moment, I thought she was going to burst into tears.

But the woman just kind of shrunk back from the doorway, poured the last of her drink down her throat and let a bright, false smile cross her lips. "No one ever comes to see me," she mumbled. "I'm just a worthless old piece of spent jet trash," then she turned and shouted, "AJ, get your worthless ass down here."

The woman then took me by the hand and led me into a large and well appointed living room with a two-story window cut into the stone wall looking out across Salt Lake. As we walked, she pressed close into my side. When she motioned me into a large, overstuffed chair, she asked, "You sure you wouldn't like a drink?" When I didn't reply she added, "If you'd like some company after you talk to AJ, just give me a shout. I so seldom have anyone to talk with here."

With that she up-ended her glass again, forgetting that she'd already emptied it, and headed for an extensive open bar at the back of the room.

CHAPTER TEN

I immediately recognized the sultry young man who entered the room after his mother had mixed herself another martini, pouring more gin over her hand than into the shaker, and departed.

He was dressed in a long black tee-shirt and jeans that hung from somewhere just north of his knees; unmistakably, the boy I'd seen push his friend out of the gondola in the Sea Fair fun zone two weeks earlier. He walked up until the toes of a pair of very pricey high-top basketball shoes on his feet were practically touching my toes, crossed his arms over his chest and gave me a sneer. He looked directly into my eyes in a challenge but didn't speak.

"My name is Dave Holman," I told the kid, "And I saw you throw Johnny Dominguez off the Ferris wheel at Sea Fair two weeks ago."

"Yeah," he barked at me, "So what are you gonna do about it, hotshot? You can't touch me and you know it. If you're a cop, you'd better go back and check with your chief before you come here hassling me again."

"You might be wrong on that," I replied softly and seriously. But I saw no fear or remorse in the arrogant look the boy shot back at me.

"You did throw Johnny Dominguez off that carnival ride?" I pressed.

"Maybe I did and maybe I didn't. What's it to you, hotshot?"

"Murder is a capital crime, son, if you weren't aware..."

"Yeah, so why don't you take it up with my dad?" The smirk grew wider. "You *know* who my dad is, don't you? So you should know that I *can* get away with murder, especially the murder of some dark alien type who shouldn't even be here in *my* country."

"I think you're a bit confused here, son. Johnny Dominguez is from right here in Texas and has... had every right to be here. You murdered him and violated his civil rights. We have laws..."

"Fuck laws!" the boy shouted, turning away from me and heading back across the room. Over his shoulder, he screamed, "My dad's a lawyer. Talk to him about laws and about people who aren't racially fit to be Texas citizens." And then he was gone.

I stood staring after him, my jaw almost resting on my chest. This child was a sick one. It sounded like the whole family was a few enchiladas short of a combination plate. I shook my head to clear it and suddenly there was his mother at my side, wrapping my left arm in both of hers.

"My name's Agnetta," she purred. "Are we ready for that drink now?"

"Thank you, Agnetta," I told her, "but, no, I have to leave now."

"Oh," she replied with a pouty face as those two black dogs came charging around the corner.

Agnetta and the dogs were headed for the bar. "I can show myself out," I told her retreating back.

As I crossed the bridge from the fortress-like structure back to my car, I heard AJ's voice shout from the castle wall above me, "Oh fuck!"

As I turned my head skyward towards the castle's battlements where young AJ paced, he screamed, "Those damn alligators have killed another one of my peacocks."

So much for getting your moral priorities in order, I thought as I got into my Saab.

CHAPTER ELEVEN

From the Laudermaelk castle, I returned to my office and asked Yolanda to do some research into the local Justice of the Peace offices, specifically what district the Laudermaelk's resided in and who was the JP for that area. It only took a handful of key strokes for my partner to bring up the information. Ames Laudermaelk resided in a narrow strip of Precinct 3 that extended out to the edge of the Salt Lake. The lady I was seeking was Dana Caruthers and she'd been re-elected to the Justice of the Peace here for the past sixteen years. According to the county website Yolanda had pulled up, the lady had an office in the Aransas County Courthouse just south of Highway 35 on Live Oak Street.

It was late afternoon, but not yet 5:00 pm, so I fired up the Saab and drove down Market to Live Oak. The courthouse was in the same complex as the Rockport Police department and the county lock-up. Dana Caruthers was just locking the door of her office to head for home.

I held out my private ticket as I approached and introduced myself. "I'm Dave Holman, a private detective investigating the death of Johnny Dominguez. Can I talk to you for a minute?"

The lady looked a little irritated, but turned the lock on her office door the other direction and motioned me inside, nodding toward the client chair as she stepped behind her desk.

I handed over one of my business cards. Dana Caruthers studied it for a moment then told me, "My office doesn't usually deal with accidental deaths, Mr. Holman, so how can I help you?"

"I don't believe Johnny Dominguez' death was an accident," I told her. "I believe he was pushed out of that Ferris wheel gondola by AJ Laudermaelk. What do you think?"

Caruthers swept her eyes around her office as though she was looking for hidden microphones or video cameras. "You know you're treading on dangerous ground here, Mr. Holman. Ames Laudermaelk has contributed a lot of money to my campaigns over the years. He swings a lot of weight in this county."

"Are you telling me that he's bought you or your office?"

A deep flush covered Dana Caruthers' face. "Nobody can buy my office!" she declared loudly. "However, I have to protect myself. Politicians have disappeared in this county. None recently, thank God, but it has been known to happen. I happen to like my job, I like serving the people."

"I'm sure you do, Ms. Caruthers, and I'm not going to share anything you might tell me. I just want to know a few things about Ames' son, AJ. Does he have any kind of juvenile record? How often has he appeared in your court?"

"Mr. Holman, you should know that juvenile records are confidential, very much so. I can't discuss anything about AJ Laudermaelk with you."

"So he *does* have a history in your court then?"

"Mr. Holman! You can get out of my office right now!"

I stood and leaned across the Justice of the Peace's desk. "Ms. Caruthers, I am investigating the brutal murder of a young boy by another young man, one of his classmates. I personally witnessed one boy throw another off a carnival ride. In spite of my testimony, the Rockport police declared it a 'death by misadventure', an accident.

"I just need to know if AJ Laudermaelk is capable of cold blooded murder. I know you've had this young man before you in court on a number of occasions. Just, please, tell me if you think AJ Laudermaelk is capable of cold blooded murder."

Dana Caruthers picked up a pencil and started beating out a crisp paradiddle on her desktop. "This is strictly off the record?" she asked. "You're not wearing some kind of recording device that can be used to get me in trouble? I have an election coming up next year and I don't want to lose this job."

"I only want to find out if Laudermaelk had a history that might point toward this kind of violent act," I replied.

Caruthers shook her head rapidly, as if to clear out some cobwebs or bad mental pictures, her blond page-boy flying out to the sides. "AJ has appeared before me many times," she rattled off in a low monotone. "Almost every time it was an assault case, an assault against some minority child, a black or Hispanic. In every case, he had a very slick attorney with him that tried to belittle the charges and excuse his client with a 'boys will be boys' argument. Even when I would recommend a harsh punishment, my decision was somehow over-ruled by some higher-up in the system and AJ received a slap on the wrist."

She closed her eyes and thought for a minute. "I'm not going to say anymore," she whispered. "And if you ever refer to me, I'll deny that we ever met. I will not testify on your behalf. This meeting never existed, Dave Holman."

"I'll agree to that," I told her, fighting to keep a grin off my face.

"AJ Laudermaelk is a dangerous child," she told me in a somewhat louder voice as we started toward her office door. "His father is even more dangerous. I'm a registered Republican, but I *do* believe in equality, that all people matter. Sometime the things I have to do in executing my office pain me. I first ran for this office thinking I could change things in this county, make the laws more fair to all our people. I still do what I can, but I've learned that there are certain obstacles we just can't fight, things that will take a lot more than an honest politician to change."

CHAPTER TWELVE

From Dana Caruthers office, I drove up Broadway to Rusty's for a beer and some time to think about what I had learned so far. I ordered a Redfish IPA and was just about to take my first sip when someone called my name from the back corner of the restaurant.

"Holman, my old California brother, how you doin'?"

It was Doctor Heffernan, sitting at a back table with his sister-in-law and her husband. "Drinkin' alone isn't good for you," the doc called. "Come on over here and join us."

"Hey, Doc," I called back, picking up my glass and heading for their table. When I'd settled in and taken a big gulp from my beer I asked, "So what do you know about local politics?"

"I try to stay out of that," the doctor told me with a grin. "Not healthy for children or other living things, as we used to say."

I let my eyes drift over his relatives seated at our table. "I'm Jen's sister," the dark haired lady across from me announced, "Laura." She extended a hand. "This is my husband, Wayde. Wayde's family has been around Rockport for generations. But I think they're staying out of politics these days. Like Michael said, it's not healthy."

"I was just curious about Ames Laudermaelk," I said with a grin. "Has he ever been any kind of local elected official?"

Doc Heffernan gave a nervous laugh while Laura and Wayde looked at each other. "Have I struck some kinda nerve?" I asked.

Wayde turned a smile my way. "The Laudermaelk/Jordan family have always figured pretty heavy in local politics," he told me, "but Ames hasn't ever held any political office, per se. He's just more kind of a, I don't know, kind of a behind the scenes guide to keep things going his way."

"His way?" I repeated, "Not the right way but his way? What do you mean by 'his way'?"

"Wayde," Laura cautioned, "you shouldn't say too much."

Wayde took a sip from a Styrofoam cup of ice tea, looked around him and said, "The Laudermaelk/Jordan family has always wanted Aransas County to maintain a high standard. Everyone knows we need a certain number of worker bees to serve in menial jobs, but the Laudermaelk's want to limit these. The communities of Rockport and Jordan are all about wealth; wealthy residents and wealthy tourist types. In the past, Ames Laudermaelk and his father did all they could to discourage blacks or people of Mexican heritage from settling here. There were, of course, old families who had been here long before Laudermaelk and Jordan had joined forces, but they were tolerated as long as they didn't bring in more of their kind.

"Then World War II came along and military veterans began to settle wherever they wanted. Ames the Second did all he could to discourage veterans of color from moving here and, at the same time, steered his son into law school so that he might be able to exercise some control over Aransas County by having a powerful lawyer, a *family* connected lawyer, on his side."

I was dumbfounded. I'd always known there was an element of prejudice in the south-eastern portion of the US, but I'd never encountered it head on until now. I wanted to ask more, but Michael Heffernan changed the subject to the shrimp wars of a few years back, when Vietnamese fisherman had started immigrating to the Jordan area. I could just guess how the Laudermaelk's felt about that.

I had another beer and listened to the conversation. I wanted to ask some questions about young AJ Laudermaelk, but the chance never came up. Just after seven, I said my goodbyes and headed for home.

CHAPTER THIRTEEN

Frustrated by the wall I seemed to be hitting, I went down to the office of The Rockport Pilot, our local twice- weekly newspaper, and took out a small classified ad. It read, "Anyone with video footage of Saturday afternoon at this year's Sea Fair between one-thirty and two p.m. I would like to review your files. Reward offered. Please call Holman Investigation at 361-727-9443." I paid for the ad to run for the next four weeks.

The weekend edition came out on Saturday and by noon Sunday, I had more than a dozen calls. Yolanda paid each respondent twenty dollars to copy their cell phone or camera video files, with a promise of fifty dollars more if the images proved helpful in our investigation.

The folks with video of Sea Fair straggled in throughout Monday and into Tuesday. Most of their footage was of family members posing before Rockport's famous Blue Crab statue or the main stage of Sea Fair's music venue.

But, after hours of searching through the files, Yolanda found two people who had either been focusing on the tall Ferris wheel or had it in the background of posing family members. The first showed some tussle in the gondola with one figure dressed all in black undoing their safety harness and grabbing his companion roughly by his shirt collar and the belt on the boy's pants. The other was quite focused on a young man struggling to regain his place against another individual trying to lift him over the gondola's side.

I contacted both of these respondents, got their addresses and drove out to give them each a check for one hundred dollars for the rights to their home movies. Both families were happy to sign a release form for me.

While I was out speaking to these folks, Yolanda was loading their footage into her computer and enhancing the files we'd captured so we might see the smallest of details about the event. She had the task completed by the time I returned.

The blown-up enhancements paid off as one of the videos gave us a very clear account of AJ the fourth grabbing Johnny Dominguez by his shirt and wrestling him around to the edge of the narrow gondola, where AJ appeared to lift Johnny's body up and over the side of the small blue Ferris wheel car. AJ Laudermaelk was wearing dark jeans and a black Slipknot tee shirt. The other boy, whom I had to assume was Johnny Dominguez, had his back to the camera.

Based on what we'd seen in our witness video, Yolanda and I sat down and built a case against AJ Laudermaelk. It didn't matter what the Rockport Police or other officials wanted to say. We had solid evidence that Ames' son had committed a murder. We were prepared to go to the highest court in the land to defend the deceased son of our client. I locked my copies of this video in my filing cabinet, knowing we had the goods for our case. When we'd reviewed what we had, Yolanda made multiple copies of the video evidence which I also locked away. I had planned to have a safe installed in the office, but hadn't gotten around to it yet. The filing cabinet should be sufficient, after all, who would be coming into our office which was also our home? Someone was here almost around the clock. Anyone trying to enter should assume that, as it's a private detective agency, we would be armed. When I got around to it, I'd put the copies in a safe deposit box in our bank.

CHAPTER FOURTEEN

The information I'd gleaned talking to local folks confirmed what I'd heard, that Ames Jordan Laudermaelk III didn't spend much time at home in Rockport. These same people told me that young Laudermaelk's mother, whom I'd met earlier, was very involved in social circles and community events that took up most of her time. AJ was an only child and a sort of wealthy latch-key kid as neither parent was there for him much of the time.

"Even when Agnetta Laudermaelk is home," one lady smiled, "She's not really there, if you know what I mean." Unfortunately, I think I did know.

AJ the fourth, it appeared, had been raised from an early age by a Hispanic nanny who doubled as a housekeeper and a Croatian gardener who also lived on the family estate out along Copano Bay.

Ames and Agnetta took time to pose with their son when he was cited for achievements at school or with the local Boy Scout troop. Laudermaelk's office sent out regular press releases to newspapers all around Texas that proved what good parents they were and how the Laudermaelk's were an exceptional Texas family. From all that appeared in the press, who could doubt that the Laudermaelk family was a model of what Texas family life should be like?

I weighed this against the evidence I had; the video of young AJ throwing his friend from the carnival ride, the mother who appeared to be totally blitzed at three in the afternoon, the fact that most of the citizens of Rockport were afraid to speak out against the Laudermaelk family, and that local law enforcement seemed inclined to turn their heads where the Laudermaelk's were concerned.

With what seemed like an airtight case, I telephoned AJ Laudermaelk the third's office in Austin and made an appointment to talk with the man. His secretary was friendly, polite and accommodating. "Ames has a few minutes Thursday afternoon between court appearances if that would work for you?"

"Yes," I told her. "My name is Dave Holman..."

"Of course," the woman chuckled. "Your name came up on our caller ID, and we *do* know who you are. Mr. Laudermaelk has been waiting to talk with you. See you on Thursday, Mr. Holman."

After setting my appointment with Laudermaelk, I started calling around to lawyers in Corpus Christi who advertised that they specialized in civil rights discrimination cases. The first four men I talked to seemed interested until A J Laudermaelk's name came up. Suddenly, their calendars were overbooked for the coming months. One man sounded outright frightened at the prospect of helping me.

I finally connected with a young man, Miles Boatwright, who thought he might be able to help me. Miles had recently moved to Texas from Boston, where he'd graduated from Harvard Law School and worked for the past seven years in a large firm learning his trade.

I started to give him some background on the Laudermaelk family, but he said he didn't need to hear it. "Either there's discrimination or there's not," he told me, "Plain and simple. We'll deal with the facts on this, not the rumors or the reputations."

I immediately liked the man and we set a date for three weeks down the line when we could meet face to face and start building our case.

I was up with the chickens Thursday morning with a few pages of notes that I studied over coffee regarding what I should say to Ames Laudermaelk. I was sure that, being a reasonable man, he would take responsibility once I told him of the evidence I had against his son.

Although I arrived twenty minutes early, I was shown right in to Laudermaelk's office. The secretary sat me down in a comfortable overstuffed chair and brought in an elaborate coffee service with a selection of coffees, teas and a tray of exotic pastries.

As soon as I'd been poured a cup of java, a door in the side of the room opened and Laudermaelk entered, shooting the cuffs on his immaculate white shirt. His suit must have cost more than my Saab had when it was new. His necktie alone probably cost more than I bill in an average week.

"I hope I haven't kept you waiting," he smiled. "I just now got out of court. I was defending a man who shot a pair of illegals whom, although he was paying them well for their service, were taking advantage of him by dealing drugs from his property. It's just a shame how these brown types think that we should be handing them the world on a silver platter."

I immediately felt uncomfortable sitting before this man. I turned my head away from his gaze and my eyes were drawn to an old framed photo plate on the wall of his office. It appeared to be a very old woodcut of four people with poles run through their bodies, the poles stuck in the ground holding their bodies upright.

He noticed me looking at the picture and said, "You're familiar no doubt with Vlad the Impaler? He was a king in Eastern Europe in the 13th century, I believe. He mastered the art of running a stake up his enemy's rear ends and through their bodies to come out of their mouths without injuring any of their vital organs or killing them. He then stuck these impaled folk's poles upright into the earth where their people would see them writhe and dance until they finally expired. He impaled thousands of his enemies like this."

I didn't know how to reply to this. Was this man putting me on or trying to intimidate me?

"The President keeps talking about a border wall to halt immigration? I know it might seem a bit cruel, but I don't think a brick-and-mortar border wall will do a lot of good. What we need to do is start impaling all the illegals we round up and putting them, on their stakes, along our southern border. That's how we can send a message they'll understand."

"A bit cruel?" I exploded. "What kind of monster are you, sir?"

Laudermaelk laughed at me. "Obviously you are the kind of California liberal my people warned me about. It's no wonder you'd want to make a martyr of my son for throwing some illegal off of a carnival ride. I don't see any crime there, but if you try to quote me on that, I'll deny everything. Mr. Holman, if we *do* build a border wall, I believe California, Oregon and Washington should also be on the other side of that wall. You're in Texas now, son. Pull your boots up and take a look at the real world.

"My son AJ, when all the dust clears, will be regarded as a hero. And we don't need panty-waist liberal poofters like you trying to sissify the great state of Texas."

I simply stared at the man. I had meant to tell him about the video evidence that I had against his son, about what I'd seen with my own eyes, but after hearing him go on with his white supremacist' views, I realized that whatever I might say would only fuel his hatred. I was dealing with a man who wasn't playing with a full moral deck. The thought occurred to me, did he see Scandinavians also as a race inferior to whatever he considered himself to be? "I'm sorry I troubled you," I told the man as I got up and headed for the door.

"Holman," he shouted at my receding frame, "don't you want to negotiate a little here? I could make it quite worth your while to forget whatever you think you saw. You might even be rewarded a very good paying position in my organization. We can always use a good investigator and I've researched your career. You seem to be a very thorough and competent detective. You just sit back down right now and let's talk."

"I don't think so," I called back over my shoulder. "I'd rather work for the devil himself." And I slammed his office door behind me, ignoring the bewildered look from his front desk girl in the lobby.

CHAPTER FIFTEEN

I was furious, talking to myself all the way back to Rockport. I couldn't believe people like Ames Jordan Laudermaelk still existed in our modern world. Didn't Texas, like California, have a largely Hispanic culture and population? I had always believed that Texas celebrated their Hispanic heritage. Mexican cuisine was everywhere. Tejano music was right up there on the charts in the southern part of the state and people worshiped the celebrities who played this Mexican-based sound.

And the Laudermaelk family had thrived in Aransas County. None of the old Mexican land owners had ever questioned or challenged their rise to power. Why would this scion of the landed gentry harbor such hate against a people who had never done anything to him or his people?

It was a mystery for which I had no answer. I decided that all I could do was keep up my fight for the truth. Maybe, if I could find all the answers, I could bring down this man with his heart full of hate. I smiled to myself as I crossed the bridge over Copano Bay and returned home to Rockport.

On the way to my office, I stopped at Spanky's Liquor Store on Business 35 for a bottle of good Scotch. I sprung the extra gold for some Speyburn single malt, feeling the need to oil my brain cells as well as possible. It was just after four in the afternoon. Normally, I would have detoured off the highway to Rusty's to have a beer or two, but today I was anxious to share my thoughts with Yolanda about the man I'd just interviewed. I wanted to get home as quickly as possible. My lady, Yolanda, had a gift for seeing through the fog and focusing on what was really out there. Hopefully, she could clear the clouds from my brain and move our investigation forward.

When I entered my office, Yolanda was waiting, seated at her computer. "Were you aware that Counselor Laudermaelk specializes in defending anti-politically correct cases? And that he's been very successful at it? He's working with the governor right now to draft legislation to abolish what they're calling sanctuary cities, where people from across the border have their rights protected. Laudermaelk has publically declared that anyone in Texas illegally must be immediately rounded up and deported, no matter what their family situation should be or who in America might be a sponsor or a family member."

"I kinda got that impression of him," I told her. "The man is a real ass-wipe." I went on to describe the picture on his wall depicting Vlad the Impaler and his views on a border wall of dying corpses. "I am going to so enjoy taking him down, no ifs, ands, or buts."

"You seem to be very upset, Dave Holman," Yolanda told me, her eyes filled with concern and focused on the scotch bottle in my hand. "Perhaps we should lie down and relax for awhile."

She locked the office door, took my hand and led me into our private apartment, where she undressed me and proceeded to massage my tense back and shoulders.

Johnny's So Long at the Fair

Almost instantly I felt better. My lady knew exactly where to touch me to make all my stress vanish. I forgot all about my expensive whiskey and must have passed out at some point during her very relaxing massage, feeling no pain.

CHAPTER SIXTEEN

I was still fast asleep later that evening when Yolanda came into our bedroom and shook my shoulder. "Dave," she whispered, "There's a hurricane building in the Gulf."

"You woke me up to tell me this?" I stated through sleep-filled eyes.

"You are not from around here," she told me. "You may not understand the seriousness of this. The weather people on Corpus Christi television say that this disturbance could become a serious threat, possibly a Category 3 hurricane, Hurricane Nathan. If it should come ashore in Rockport, it could do major damage all over the area."

"Oh, please," I told her. "Surely hurricanes don't come to places like Rockport. Come on to bed, get to sleep and don't bother me again."

I went about my business the next day, making a trip to Corpus Christi for some office supplies. The sky was a cloudless, bright blue and the winds were calm. I turned on the public radio station when my compact disc of Chet Baker finished. They were also talking about this storm heading directly for the Texas coast, a tropical depression for now but, they said, it could become a Category 1 hurricane by the time it made landfall, somewhere between Corpus Christi and Port La Vaca, two cities that bookended Rockport along our Gulf Coast.

Back in Rockport, at a stoplight on Market Street just before turning into my office, Lisa, a friend who owns an art gallery on Austin Street in old town Rockport, pulled up beside my Saab, rolled down the window of her truck and asked, "Are you planning to ride it through or are you leaving town?"

When I gave her a blank look, she replied, "Hurricane Nathan. Are you planning to leave town?"

As the light changed to green I shouted that I wasn't sure. I remembered watching Hurricane Katrina hit New Orleans some years ago on the television of a brew pub in Oslo, Norway, where I was vacationing. But that was New Orleans, a good distance north of Rockport.

As I was pulling into the lot in front of my office, the announcer on my car radio was saying that Rockport was under a mandatory evacuation order. They played a tape of the mayor of our town telling citizens that if they weren't planning on leaving town, they should take a permanent marker and write their name and social security number on their forearm so their dead bodies could be identified. Political scare tactics, I thought to myself as I mounted the stairs to my office.

When I opened my eyes the next morning there was a strange tension in the air. Yolanda's computer screen showed videos of everyone running around like chickens with their legs cut off. The news predicted that Nathan would come ashore near Rockport by late afternoon as a category 3 or 4, a major storm.

This California boy still didn't buy into the fury. I'd survived major earthquakes and fire storms back home in Los Angeles. What more could a hurricane have to offer?

Yolanda told me that her uncle had a place near Austin where we could evacuate to. It was owned by the Elephant Rescue, so we wouldn't have to pay anything.

Again, I guffawed at my partner. A hurricane was just a lot of wind and rain, nothing we should fear. "We'll stay right here and we'll be just fine!" I declared. I sat in my office without a care, going over the files on my case and planning how I could help an attorney defend my client to prove that their child had been maliciously murdered by the son of a radical, racist politician, and how my new lawyer friend, Miles, would help me ruin the man with his Neanderthal racial views.

By around six in the evening, I became aware of the winds howling outside my windows. It was a horrifying screech. I called to Yolanda, but she was busy wrapping cling film around our filing cabinets and desk drawers.

An hour or so later, the walls seemed to be pulsing with the changing barometric pressure outside. Shortly after that, the lights went out, but the powerful wind continued to increase.

"Time to go, Dave," Yolanda whispered, taking my hand.

"Go where?" I asked.

"Anywhere but here," she breathed holding up a large battery-powered lantern. As the lights flickered on again and then flashed out, I stubbornly remained at my desk listening to the howling wind, which was now accompanied by thunder and pounding rain.

The rain lashed our windows and the wind sang a dreadful, mournful song for an hour or more. With no electric power, I could do nothing but sit and wonder if I'd made the right decision.

I played Yolanda's lantern light over my notes as I added more thoughts on my case.

Then the noise outside suddenly subsided into a deathly quiet. I smiled at my partner with an "I told you so" grin. The worst was over, just as I had predicted.

"Now that wasn't so bad, was it," I grinned.

"Dave Holman, you big dolt," Yolanda screamed at me, punching me hard in my right shoulder, "That was only the prelude. We've just entered the eye of the storm! When these few minutes of calm pass, we're in for the worst fury that this storm has to offer. How else can I make you understand? This storm will kill us both if we don't get out of here."

"Okay, so let's head out to Austin then."

"Dave, you idiot," she shouted from a face blotchy with red spots of worry or anger, "it's too late to go anywhere. We have to find some shelter from the wind and rain right now."

I looked at my partner with naked confusion as the wind increased once more.

"Follow me," she shouted.

I grasped Yolanda's hand and she led me down the steps and into the feed and fence store on the first floor of our building. The door was unlocked. It appeared that our landlord's staff had left in a big hurry. They'd even taken the two parrots and a handful of cats that usually patrolled the business.

As the wind continued to increase and heavy rain began falling outside once more, we buried ourselves in a bin of hay that was for sale to local ranches. Yolanda and I clung to each other as the wind and pounding rain went beyond anything I'd ever heard, like some kind of Maynard Ferguson trumpet solo two octaves above any sound previously played. I don't know how long we stayed like that before the howl of wind and paradiddle of rain began to quiet. I perked up at the reduced fury and stood to go explore, certain that the worst must have passed by now.

"No, Dave, stay here with me," Yolanda pleaded.

"Oh come on, the storm is over," I told her.

"Dave Holman," she scolded. "Do you know nothing of tropical storms? There may be tornados or other anomalies out there. We just don't know what nature has in store. "

I was about to protest when the ceiling above gave a groan and much of my office on the second floor fell around the bin of straw where we'd taken refuge. We were only spared because of a pole and chain link cage surrounding the bin holding the straw in which we huddled.

CHAPTER SEVENTEEN

Yolanda and I clung together in our straw haven until we could see the sun coming up outside. I stood first and held my hand out to her. Together, we walked out through the double-wide front door frame, though we needn't have bothered, as the walls were gone on either side of the portal. Looking up once outside, I noticed that much of our second story apartment was gone. The outside staircase was still standing, but it led to the empty heavens with no floor at its upper end. The RV park next door looked as though someone had taken a giant spatula and turned everything upside down, with a few of the motor homes exploded into splinters of wood and scattered clothing.

My Saab appeared untouched, but Yolanda's VW Thing with the Elephant Rescue logos on the doors had been carried on the wind into a large oak tree which had, subsequently, landed on the roof of a tin commercial building partway down the block.

Driven by my amazement, I led Yolanda on a walk through ankle deep water down Market Street. Some of the familiar businesses just weren't there anymore. Others were twisted or flattened into the landscape. The giant tire outlet a few blocks east of us was standing, but its tin roof had blown off and now blocked all four lanes of Market Street.

When I finally caught my breath and connected with my senses, I turned to Yolanda.

"Austin?" I asked.

"A bit late," she retorted. "We'd better get on the road as quickly as we can. That is, if the road is still there."

At this point, my investigation was so far from my thoughts that I didn't give the evidence I'd gathered or anything else a second thought. I had just over half a tank of gas in the Saab, which was fortunate as the gas stations along Market Street lay in ruin. I simply prayed that there would be someplace open along the way where we could fill the tank, and maybe get some breakfast and coffee, lots of coffee.

With a clearer head than mine, Yolanda took a few minutes to find her laptop computer in the wreckage, carry it to the car and strap it into the back seat with one of the seat belts. "I don't want to be out of touch," she smiled at me when I gave her a funny look.

"You think it still works? I asked.

"Let's just say I'm putting a big bet on it," she replied with a hopeful smile.

All through Rockport it looked like we were traveling in a war zone. Much of the city crouched in ruins. Our lovely and honored old oak trees had crushed many of the homes we passed and blocked doors or windows to trap residents inside their structures.

We had started up Texas 35 toward Tivoli and Victoria when the radio informed us that Nathan had already taken that path. I did a quick U-turn and we headed for Highway 181 and San Antonio instead.

It took the entire day to reach Austin with the detour through San Antonio and heavy rains we encountered along the way. We lived on coffee and doughnuts, the only food we could get at our stops to fill the gas tank. It was nearly dark outside when we reached the Elephant Rescue Ranch complex. Yolanda's Uncle Jishnu was there at the ranch's main building to greet us.

"I was expecting you two days ago," he scolded my lady. "What happened?"

"My fault," I breathed at him with a humble face. "I guess I just didn't understand about hurricanes."

"You put my niece's life in danger?" he began, his composure as close to angry as I'd ever seen this passive Buddhist man.

"It is okay, Uncle." Yolanda defended. "The compassionate Buddha protected us and everything so far has turned out alright."

Jishnu took a deep breath that turned into a smile. "You are right, my child," he told her. "Everything happens as it should. Please forgive my moment of anger. Please let me show you to your rooms. We will be serving dinner in the main hall soon, but you have at least an hour to get settled in first." Uncle Jishnu put his hands together in front of his chest, as if in prayer. "Namaste," he smiled with a slight bow.

CHAPTER EIGHTEEN

The first thing my lady did when we entered our room was plug her laptop into the wall and press the power button. We both held our breath while we waited for the light and hum which would tell us the machine was still alive. The box was slow booting up, but eventually Yolanda's home page filled the small screen.

Before checking email or anything else, the lady clicked on the icon for my evidence files. My notes for the case and our evidence videos all opened. With a sigh of relief, we shut down the computer. All we had were the clothes on our back but we shed them and both took long hot showers as if to wash the storm out of our systems. When I came out of the bathroom wrapped in a large and fluffy white towel, Yolanda held out a pile of items.

"One of Jishnu's elephant boys is close to your size," she told me. "See if these will fit you."

There was a pair of jeans that came down to my mid-ankles and a blue Hawaiian shirt covered in dancing pachyderms, along with socks and a pair of white boxer shorts. I normally prefer y-fronts, but I was glad of the clean underwear and the other items. Later, we could put our soiled 'Nathan' clothes through the wash and get more comfortably dressed. Yolanda had some old outfits that she'd left at the rescue ranch for when she visited the animals that stayed there, so her emergency garments fit much better then what I'd been given.

Jishnu served us a wonderful meal of prawn curry and stewed spinach with chunks of cottage cheese. After our meal, we sampled some fine brandy and turned on the television to see just how bad Hurricane Nathan had left our coastal abode. There were home videos of Jordan Beach and downtown Rockport submitted by residents who had rode out the storm, accompanied by warnings about the dangers of entering damaged structures. The local Austin TV anchor lady stated that the National Guard was imposing a dusk to dawn curfew. Only people with a picture ID showing a local address would be allowed to enter Aransas County, and then only between 6:00 am and 6:00 pm.

After some commercials, the next segment of the news featured an interview with Rockport's police chief warning about looters in the area. The few police units left to patrol the area had already arrested half a dozen people going through the wreckage and stealing belongings from damaged structures.

I immediately sat bolt upright. "I, I've got to get back to Rockport," I stuttered.

"Dave Holman," Yolanda chuckled. "Do you think someone in hillbilly central is going to steal your modern jazz records or compact discs? Like they'd even know what they were."

"No," I replied with a worried face, "the evidence we collected. Looters don't have to be poor people trying to make a buck. Someone like Ames Laudermaelk would be clever enough to see an opportunity to ruin my case against him. He would have local minions who would do his bidding and go through the wreckage of our place. He may have already taken the opportunity to search our files. I've got to get back right away."

"Dave, you know I have copies of everything saved on my hard drive. And, my computer is right here with us. Would it really be worth a trip back to all that devastation just to check on your original evidence?"

"Yolanda," Uncle Jishnu pleaded, "You will remain here with us, will you not? It would be crazy to go back to a place with no fresh water or electricity. Let Dave Holman take his chances, child. You don't have to be part of his madness."

Yolanda's face clouded. I watched as many different emotions crossed her eyes. In the end, she gave a weak smile.

"I'm sorry, Uncle. My place is with Dave. If he believes that it's important to return he will need me to help sort this all out."

Yolanda re-belted her computer into the rear seat of my Saab. If need be, we could rent or buy a generator for electric power. Neither of us stopped to think that there would be no internet connections when we returned to Rockport. As soon as our original set of clothes were dry, we started up my motor and headed back to Rockport.

We drove back the way we'd come through San Antonio, tuned to a Corpus Christi radio station much of the way. As it wasn't quite sunrise when we approached the coast, and remembering the dusk to dawn curfew, we checked into a La Quinta Inn just north of Corpus Christi. We were both nearly dead on our feet anyway. A few hours of sleep would do us a world of good.

We woke up three hours too late to take advantage of the hotel's free breakfast bar, but we sucked up the in-room instant coffee before hitting the hot and dusty. We stopped at an undamaged International House of Pancakes in Portland on our way home.

From Portland, we started to notice the wide path of damage up Texas Highway 35, things we hadn't paid attention to in our hurry to leave town the day before. Advertising billboards lay beside the roadway in ruin. RV parks along the four lane looked as though a large hand had been drawn across them to clear the board of some giant game. A new car dealership beside the highway was missing part of its façade and new trucks were piled in a heap at the end of the paved forecourt. Most of the road signs with speed warnings and exit markings were bent over backwards and unreadable.

We almost missed our exit for Market Street as the sign had been blown away by the storm and the landscape so changed as to be almost unrecognizable. The stop signs were gone when we exited the main highway and parts of buildings, along with old oak trees, were scattered over Market Street. I pulled into our parking lot just as the remaining section of our former apartment swayed and then fell into the rubble of the first floor feed and fence store.

CHAPTER NINETEEN

I bounded out of the Saab to search the rubble for my filing cabinet which contained all my case notes as well as the original video clips I'd obtained of young Johnny being thrown from the Sea Fair Ferris wheel. Halfway up the porch steps that led to the ruin of our building a state trooper appeared from around a corner to block my path.

"I'm sorry, sir," he told me through a tight-set jaw. "This building is very unstable and could collapse at any minute. You saw how a part of the wall here just fell. I can't let you enter these premises."

When I started to protest that this had been my office, the man reached for the handcuffs on his belt. "Please, step away from the structure," he barked. "I don't want to have to arrest you."

I stared at him belligerently for a few short seconds until I felt Yolanda grab my shoulder and tug me back toward our car.

"It's not worth getting nicked, Dave," she said loudly, then with a smile she told the policeman, "Please understand, this is a very emotional time and we're very stressed and upset right now."

That brought a small smile to the patrolman's lips. "I understand, ma'am. I'm just doing my duty. We have enough people in Rockport injured already and we don't want any more folks crushed by falling rubble. Do you need me to direct you to a shelter?"

Unsure just how to proceed, I told the man that we had a motel in Corpus Christi. "We just came back to retrieve some important legal papers… Like insurance documents? If I could just go in for a moment to locate my filing cabinet?"

The state cop's smile went back into a frown. "Like I told you, no one will be entering this building. State Disaster Relief is setting up an emergency center on Magnolia Street, by the old HEB market. They can help you connect with your insurance people."

I gave the man a questioning look but Yolanda pulled me farther back toward the Saab once more, whispering, "Dave, be cool. Maybe we can sneak back later, after curfew… like, under cover of darkness. Let's go back to the motel in Corpus now. I'll bet they have a business center with an Internet connection there so we can do some checking on line."

The state patrolman assumed a parade-rest stance on the porch of our building, almost challenging me to try and get past him either through or around the standing door frame. I turned and went back to the car, sliding into the driver's seat and shooting him a broad, false smile.

As I started the engine and put the vehicle in reverse, I asked Yolanda what she thought we should do now.

"If we come back after the curfew," I pointed out, "we risk being shot as looters. How about we park down the block and wait for Mr. Guard-dog to leave."

As I said it, I noticed two or three other police units cruising Market Street from both directions, keeping an eye on local business structures.

"Dave," Yolanda scolded. "I have copies of most your notes in my computer along with the film clips you were given. I'll bet any new notes you've taken are in the notebook you carry in your pocket. What is so urgent that we should risk our lives to enter a building that might fall on us, not to mention being arrested?"

"Mostly," I told my partner, "that I need to know if anyone has been tampering with my evidence. We've been away for almost two days. Ames' people could easily have gone in right after we left and made copies of everything I know. That would give him a huge leg-up if any of this ever goes to court."

Yolanda laughed her musical laugh. "Dave Holman, I think you sound totally paranoid. Do you think someone, anyone, would be waiting for a natural disaster with a plan to creep your office if it should happen to cave in? Just listen to yourself."

I had to laugh along with her. I was sounding pretty crazy, after all. Nobody knew this tropical storm would grow so quickly into a major event, let alone that it would come ashore right in our little seaside village.

"Do you think B J's Brewery in Corpus survived the hurricane?" I inquired. "If it's still standing, we can discuss this over a beer and some pizza."

"Drive on, Captain," Yolanda giggled, lightly punching my shoulder.

CHAPTER TWENTY

O ver a Lagunita's IPA at BJ's Brewery, Yolanda explained to me that she had copied my case notes to something she called a 'cloud,' a big computer storage place somewhere out in space, in addition to saving them on her hard drive.

"From the motel's business center or anywhere else, we can safely view whatever you want from your case notes. I'll bet you can even print copies of everything, though they'll probably charge you an arm and a leg for the paper. We don't even have to unpack my computer."

"And the videos?" I asked her.

"Do you really need those before you can get the cops to listen or your clients are ready to file a motion with the court? You can certainly watch those files as often as you like from the cloud to build your case."

"And no one else can see what's on this 'cloud' thing?"

"It's password protected, Dave. And I'm the only one that knows the password." She laughed that musical laugh again, "Hell, Dave, I'm the only one who even knows it's *on* the cloud."

We imbibed a second beer while Yolanda explained to me how Internet 'clouds' worked and how secure all our data was in this never-never land in the sky. I was more than a bit skeptical, but I wanted to trust my lady.

"So what can we do tomorrow to move the case forward?" I pressed my lady. "I don't think I can just sit in a motel room and go through 'could'a maybe' plots in my head."

Yolanda tossed back her dark hair and laughed. "Dave Holman, you're supposed to be the detective here. You know there's a lot we can do between the curfew hours back in Rockport.

"Did the Dominguez family stay behind to ride out the storm?" she continued. "If so, are they still at their home in the area, living without electricity or water? And if they're there, can they give you more names of possible witnesses or other people we can contact to back the idea that AJ is a racist?

"And what about your psychologist friend, Dr. Heffernan? If he's still in Rockport, maybe he can help you build a profile of the kid we suspect of the murder while we're waiting."

I felt like a total nerd for not thinking of these things but then I'd never been through a hurricane before. My mind was more than a bit scrambled. I'd ridden through plenty of earthquakes with major damage, but nothing like we'd just survived here on the Texas coast. What the heck, at least what my lady proposed would keep me from sitting in a tiny motel room slowly going crazy.

We ordered a large pizza and another round of drinks then sat there for much of the afternoon. Driving out of the pizza place, I noticed an open Half-Price Bookstore in the center that advertised music and video as well as reading material.

We escaped reality for an hour or more perusing the various entertainment media the shop offered. We didn't have a player or a television to watch DVDs, but there were some amazing compact discs there at a very reasonable price. I purchase Charlie Parker with Strings, although I knew I already had a copy somewhere, and a live recording of Coleman Hawkins from the late fifties. Who knew if I'd ever see my own collection of jazz music again when the debris of Nathan was cleared? If nothing else, we could listen to these discs in my car or on Yolanda's laptop.

The next morning we got an early start. We watched the sun rise driving over the Corpus Christi Bay Bridge and arrived in Portland just as they were opening the doors at the International House of Pancakes restaurant.

After a big breakfast, we got the waitress to fill our thermos with coffee and motored out onto Texas 181 toward Rockport.

The highway still seemed unfamiliar, like something from a half-remembered dream. Once again we nearly missed the Rockport exit. My mind boggled that we'd even found our home the day before.

We drove past the ruin of our office into the old historic district of Rockport. I hung a U-turn near the Market Street fishing pier and turned right up Austin Street. Again, I was totally lost. Much of the main drag was simply gone, as though it had never been there.

After a sweep up Austin Street to the old HEB, where the first responders and rescuers had set up their command post, we backtracked to Market and went back along that street, beyond the Texas 35 freeway. To the west, the devastation seemed even worse. The Bottle Brothel was standing, but its roof hung from a stand of oak trees behind the parking area. Betsy sat on the ruined porch of the store with her shotgun in her lap, ready to ward off looters.

I pulled into the lot and hailed her.

"Dave Holman," she greeted me with a grimace. "Why weren't you here to ward off all this wind and water?

"You were here through the storm?" I replied.

"Where else could I go?" she glared back at me. "This business is my life. I tried to send my girls home, but many of them were scared to leave. They're bunked out in the back storage area."

"Anything I can do?" I began, to which she raised her shotgun and told me, "Just go away. I'll call you when I'm ready to deal with people, any people. Even friends like you. Right now I'm just too depressed and so are my girls."

Beyond Betsy's, things got worse. Houses that had been built on stilts now lay on the ground in piles of wood, wallboard and furniture. Tract style homes were torn in half or simply flattened. One home, built from an old geodesic dome, stood undamaged among the rubble.

We found the Dominguez family cowered in a red and blue camping tent in what had been the driveway of their home, and was now simply a pile of sticks and stones. The family all had a vacant, shell-shocked look about them, like 'is this really happening to us? Right on top of losing our son, we should lose everything else that mattered in our lives?'

I got out of the car and approached them slowly. When I got close, Melba crawled out of the tent.

"Do you have any water we can buy?" she asked with pitiful, dark eyes.

Yolanda immediately got out of the Saab and went back to the trunk of the car where she found a couple warm plastic bottles of H2O, which she tossed to Melba along with Jessie, who had followed her out of the tent.

"Do you have any food here for yourselves?" my partner asked them.

"A few dozen tortillas," Jessie called back after draining his bottle of water.

"We manage to pick out the moldy bits," Melba added. "Same as with the cheese we rescued before the refrigerator got too hot."

"There're some church groups giving out bottled water and hot meals, along with military MREs, Meals Ready to Eat, in the old HEB parking lot. Why haven't you gone to town?" Then I followed Jessie's eyes as they traveled into a close by stand of old oak trees where the family pick-up truck lay on its side under a fallen tree trunk almost as big around as their vehicle.

"Oh man!" I uttered. "I'm so sorry."

Yolanda and I excused ourselves and backtracked to the Rockport Historic district where we loaded up the Saab with cases of bottled water, a palate of MREs and some tacos right off the grill of one of the charity groups by the roadside. We also bought a Styrofoam cooler from a vender along the highway which we filled with ice from an open filling station that had a series of generators hooked up to their ice machine. The price was twice what it should have been, but no one had much choice at this point.

The Dominguez's were thrilled with the gifts we brought back to them. "You can add this to our bill when you've finished your investigation," Jessie assured me.

"Fat chance, my friend," I answered back," Right now, you need to survive, to get strong and to rebuild your life. I'll do all I can to help you and I don't want to hear anything about paying me back.

"If you need to rent a car or truck to get around, I'll gladly drive you to any open car rental agency between here and Corpus. You might be a client, Jessie, but you're also a valuable friend. And I do all I can to help my friends."

CHAPTER TWENTY-ONE

We got Jessie and Melba into a rental truck from an agency in Corpus Christi with enough time to spare that they could drive to the disaster relief center in Rockport's historic district before nightfall. While we were there, Yolanda also rented a vehicle, a small Fiat convertible, to replace her Elephant Rescue VW thing until we had time to shop for a new car for her charity.

From the rental agency we decided to have a look around Corpus Christi to see what kind of damage Nathan had left along the bay front. I drove out the Cross-Town Expressway and pulled off the highway into the old waterfront of Corpus. Television news reports at our hotel had said the city had also suffered damage but I hadn't noticed much yet.

Cruising down Mesquite Street near the water, I couldn't see anything like we'd witnessed in Rockport. A few traffic signals and street signs lay by the side of the road and we saw some broken windows, along with bits of debris blown from building facades, but I could see no collapsed structures or roofless buildings.

Then around Williams Street, to the left of us, I noticed a glowing red sign advertising the Rebel Toad Brewery. I circled the block and parked the Saab beneath the brew pub's marquee.

When we entered and sat at the bar, I looked around. "You seem to have come through Nathan pretty well."

"There's a special God that protects people brewing beer and ale," the dark haired lady behind the bar laughed. "I only wish our house had fared so well."

"Next time there's a storm threatening we'll start brewing a batch of ale," Yolanda told her with a straight face.

For the next few hours, we escaped the post Nathan stress, drinking what the Rebel Toad folks called Haywire IPA, a strong ale with a decent kick to it, and talking to other folks who had survived the recent storm.

Yolanda took the wheel of the Saab to guide us back to our hotel while I sat back and ruminated on hurricanes and other natural disasters. Back in our rented digs, I crashed heavily as soon as my head hit the pillow.

I woke up once in the night in a state of confusion, finally remembering where I was and finding my way to the bathroom to unload the beer from my system. After that I had a few terrible dreams, more to do with faceless men carrying guns chasing me than hurricanes.

The next time I opened my eyes, bright sunlight was flooding our room. The bedside clock said it was just after 10:00 and there was a note propped up beside the digital clock screen.

"Gone down to get some free breakfast," Yolanda had written in her firm, neat hand. "I'll bring you back something."

With a clouded brain, I dragged myself under the room's shower, toweled off, and without bothering to find my clothes, headed for the in-room coffee machine.

Johnny's So Long at the Fair

I was standing there with a towel loosely circling my waist and sipping hot java when Yolanda entered the room.

"Dave Holman," she exclaimed. "I could have been the maid coming to clean the room! Do you have no shame?"

"I think I have a bit of a hangover," I confessed. "Didn't you have a 'do not disturb' card to hang on the door when you left?"

My lady giggled at that. "Well, yeah, I did hang the sign on the doorknob. I was just testing you."

I sat at the room's wide desk and ate the bagel my lady had brought me. When I finished that I was still hungry. I figured we'd stop somewhere for a real breakfast when we got going.

CHAPTER TWENTY-TWO

After we turned off South Padre Island Drive toward Rockport we found a Denny's coffee shop along Interstate 37 just past an old dog racing track. I knew Denny's from California although I didn't know that the chain had found their way into Texas. Rumors I'd heard said the franchise had almost gone out of business.

I had one of their cheap combo breakfasts with eggs, potatoes and some kind of doughy cake product. Yolanda just ordered a stack of pancakes and hardly ate any of them before pushing her plate away.

By noon we were back on the familiar road to what remained of Rockport. I had it on my schedule to interview a couple other members of the Dominguez family whom Jessie had mentioned as knowing Johnny well.

I also planned to check on Dr. Heffernan, to see if he'd survived the storm and then to ask him some questions about the so-called accident at Sea Fair. I was willing to pay the good doctor his usual rates as a consultant if he could give me some insight into young AJ and his personality. I knew I could bill it to my client and the court would award them enough in damages to cover the expense.

But would the good doctor be willing to talk with me? Before Hurricane Nathan had struck, when I'd had a beer or two with him at Rusty's, Doc had indicated that he wanted nothing to do with local politics and I'd gotten the feeling that he, like many others, was afraid of Ames Laudermaelk. What did this man have over so many local people?

Yolanda nudged me when we approached the Market Street exit into Rockport. I still couldn't recognize our community in Nathan's aftermath. I turned right onto Market Street and began a slow cruise, cautious of the wreckage and debris piled on either side of the four-lane road.

Two blocks down, my eye caught sight of a large rental van backed into the parking area of the feed and fence store where my office had been on the building's second floor.

There was a state trooper standing outside the wreckage of the property while two men in overalls were loading much of the debris of my office into the back of the truck. They didn't seem to be bothering with clothing, CDs or vinyl records. Files and loose papers appeared to be their target.

I pulled the Saab right up to the trooper's knees before I stopped.

"What the hell is going on here?" I shouted into the state cop's face. "Who gave you the right to carry away my personal property?"

"May I see some ID please," he spit back at me, his face a mask of indifference.

I opened my wallet to show my driver's license on the upper flap and my Private Investigator's card just below it.

"As you can see, this is my address. And, all the papers your men are taking away are my personal property relating to my professional work, including current investigations which

I'm pursuing. So can you kindly call off your men and let me go through my papers before they've loaded any more of my office into your U-Haul?"

"I'm sorry, Mr. Holman, sir," the man replied, without a hint of a smile or any other human expression. "I'm just following orders from the governor's office. I don't know why we've been told to collect these things, and frankly, it's not my business to care. I just follow orders. Maybe the state is placing it in safe storage for you while the structure gets demolished."

"Then how come no one has notified me about it?"

"I can't say," the patrolman told me, his lips beginning to twitch toward a smile. "Like I said, I'm just following orders. I don't like being assigned to play some kind of security guard in this disaster zone, but when my major tells me what to do, I do it without complaining or wondering why, Period."

"And what is your name and your major's name?" I asked, "Because I intend to file a complaint in this matter."

The man mechanically reached into the pocket of his uniform blouse and extracted a business card. "My office can give you my commanding officer's name if they want to. I'm not authorized to give out that information." He then turned away, dismissing me with his quiet motion. The card he had handed me said he was Patrolman Ralph Hughes. The address on the card was the Austin DPS Barracks, on South Interstate 35 at W. William Cannon Drive.

I returned to the Saab with anger brimming just below the surface. "Dave," Yolanda said soothingly, rubbing my neck and shoulders with her left hand, "Don't blow your cool now. It isn't worth having a stroke over this."

"He said he had orders from the governor," I hissed, "The *republican* governor, who is probably a close buddy of Ames Laudermaelk. You know why they're collecting my papers."

Yolanda turned in her seat to face forward. I could see a tear forming in her left eye. "I'm sorry, Dave, I truly am."

CHAPTER TWENTY-THREE

From Market Street, we drove up the road along Little Bay to Jordan Beach. As we entered Jordan, I could see more extensive damage. The Lighthouse Inn's trademark lighthouse lay half in Jordan Bay. On the other side of the road, Rusty's was still standing, but half the roof was gone along with the outdoor patio and deck where live musicians had performed most nights. On the next block, entire buildings were reduced to rubble; a fish market, a senior center, a barber shop and another restaurant.

Beyond the business district, we turned left for one block, then right, into the doctor's driveway.

Doc's wife, Jen, was tending to some flowers in the garden by the front porch of their residence. I introduced her to Yolanda and the ladies had a brief conversation about how many plants had survived while tall trees had been ripped from their roots.

"Speaking of large trees," Jen told us, "We had one come right through our roof."

Jen invited us into the house, offering us drinks. Walking through the living room, I noticed a number of blue tarps hanging from the ceiling with puddles of water flowing from beneath them. As we declined refreshments, a loud roar came from beyond the kitchen and Dr. Michael appeared. His hair was sticking out from his head as though he had stuck his finger into an electrical socket. He was very drunk and not happy to have company. Waving a vodka bottle around, he told us he wasn't in the mood to talk to anyone. I mentioned that I wanted to hire him as a consultant for the case I was working on, but he only wanted to hold forth about how his neighbor's tree had come through his roof and destroyed his home.

Jen hurried us back out to my car. She apologized for the good doctor, telling us that they had ridden out the storm and it had made Michael a little crazy. She promised to call when things were more normal. "I know Michael will want to work with you on your case when he feels better," she told us. "He has often said that he would like to be more involved in things like detective work. Did he ever tell you that he used to have a private investigator's license?"

From Jordan Beach, we drove away from the coast along Copano Bay to the address Jesse Dominguez had given us. Out here to the west of Rockport, the devastation seemed much worse. Maybe it was the flat open plain that allowed the wind to do more damage. What had been large, expensive homes were now unrecognizable piles of rubble.

Johnny Dominguez's grandmother rented an RV just off the highway that ran along the bay. Melba had told us that her mother probably knew Johnny even better than they did. When Johnny had questions or problems, he would usually consult his Grandma Rose before bringing his issues to his parents. She was a kind and understanding lady, Jesse had told me. She had wisdom she claimed came from an old ancestor who was a Cherokee native, although all the records they could find simply listed her as Mexican.

We found Rose Dominguez in her small trailer that had been, according to her, spun around 180 degrees by the storm, but remained upright and undamaged.

Before we got out of the Saab, a dark, heavy-set woman with flashing green eyes came out of the recreational vehicle and stepped toward us. "You must be Dave Holman," she smiled. "Jesse said you'd be coming to see me. I'm ready to do all I can to help you find who murdered my favorite grandson."

We followed her into her mobile home where we were greeted by loud hissing from a tiger striped ginger cat with fur standing on end and a tail swishing rapidly to and fro.

I wasn't sure how to proceed but Yolanda reached a hand down and stroked the orange cat, which immediately began to purr and rub herself against my partner's leg.

"That's Tabby Wynette," Rose announced with a wink.

"Tabby Wynette?" I asked.

"She whines all the time!" Rose told us with a giggle. "Johnny loved Tabby. They had a special thing together."

Rose told us she had a fresh pot of coffee on the stove. "Can I pour you each a cup? Or perhaps you'd prefer some herbal tea?"

"We're good," I told the woman, after which Yolanda inquired as to what flavor of herbal tea.

"I've got hibiscus, chamomile or mint," Rose answered, putting water into a stainless steel kettle and carrying it just outside her door to a small fire in half an oil drum.

"Chamomile sounds lovely," my partner called after her. "Dave, are you sure you don't want a cup of coffee?"

I thought for a minute and then relented when Rose came back inside. "Yes, I guess I would like a cup, with just a drip of milk if you could."

"It'll have to be powdered milk," the old lady laughed. "No refrigerator."

Rose ushered us into wooden chairs with red cushions on the seats set around her mobile home's drop-down kitchen table.

When Yolanda and I had sat down, sipped our beverages and complemented our hostess, I got down to business.

"So what can you tell me about Johnny?" I asked. "Did he seemed to be depressed or in any way unstable enough that he might have jumped from a Ferris wheel?"

"Johnny loved life," Rose stated emphatically. "He was definitely not the type to take his own life. Anyone saying different doesn't know my grandson. I'll swear to that in any court anywhere."

I wasn't sure how to reply to that. So far everything we had heard screamed that Johnny Dominguez was a good and stable young man. On the other hand, A J Laudermaelk appeared to be an unstable child with lots of issues. The profile we'd gathered on him showed him to be a bully; a young man who felt he was privileged and could do whatever he liked with no regard for the consequences. That, coupled with his father's racist views, gave me a lot to think about.

"Johnny was a sensitive child," Grandma Rose told us. "He carried a large pad of paper around with him and was always sketching birds and animals. Some of his sketches he later turned into watercolors. He also played the clarinet in the high school orchestra.

"He wasn't real interested in sports. That was a sore spot with AJ and some of the macho boys. They called him things like 'queer bait' because he didn't want to play football or basketball. He also refused to defend himself when the bullies would attack him. Instead, he would go to the school police and file complaints against his tormentors, which didn't do much to increase his popularity, but he had his own circle of friends. The smarter children admired Johnny for his intellect and his creative abilities."

"Did Johnny have any close or special friends?" I asked the woman.

"He had a good friend last year. Ron was a senior, one year ahead of Johnny. They sat next to each other in the school orchestra. Ron used to stick up for Johnny, but after he graduated, Ron moved to Austin to attend the university there. Johnny did have a sort of girlfriend, Savannah. I don't know how serious it was, but they spent a lot of time together. He called her 'Vanna.' She was into modern dance, according to Johnny."

"Do you know her last name," I asked, "or how I might locate her?"

Rose gave me a puzzled look. "I think her family lived in an apartment in Rockport. Johnny never said much about it except that her family was poor. He was embarrassed for her. He always changed the subject when I asked about her family."

"Anything you could find about her would be a help," I told Rose. "I really need to speak to her and to Johnny's friend, Ron, as well."

"Ron I can help with," Rose smiled. "I know his parents from the Rockport Democratic Society. Randy and Beth Burreson live by the country club. I'm sure they'd be happy to talk with you. Maybe they know more about this girl Savannah."

Rose turned and rummaged for a minute or two in a kitchen drawer near her hard-wired wall phone.

"Here it is," she exclaimed facing us again with a red notebook in her hand. "The Burreson's live on Oak Bay Road, just off the golf course." She wrote down their address and telephone number on a blank page in her notebook, tore it out and handed it to me. "I know they'll want to help."

Then Rose brought a photo album from a shelf just outside the kitchen area and showed us photographs of Johnny from a small boy through the high school's band recital a few months ago, while we finished our coffee and tea.

"You might want to check with my other son, Vince," Rose called after us as we were heading back to the Saab.

I turned back to her. "You have another son?"

"Vince and Jesse didn't always see eye-to-eye," the grandmother said with her head down and in a soft tone. "Vince is a fisherman. It's supposed to be just a hobby, but my youngest son would much rather fish than work. Jesse always calls him a ne'r-do-well and won't have much to do with his brother. It has caused me a lot of pain in my heart over the years, but Johnny was very fond of his

Uncle Vince. Sometime Johnny would ditch school to go out on Vince's boat for the day.

"Johnny very likely told Vince things he would never tell me… boy things, or man things. You know how it is when young men begin to mature and discover girls." She gave a nervous giggle.

"Yeah, I can understand that," I answered. "So where can we find this Uncle Vince?"

"I think he's living aboard an old shrimp boat these days," Rose told us. "That's the first place I'd look for him, I mean if the boat is in port."

"And by 'in port,' you mean?"

"Jordan Harbor," Grandma Rose laughed. "Behind Charlotte Plumber's Restaurant, third boat down to the left from the commercial craft advertising Sand Hill Crane tours. I believe it's called Laid Back. It would have Laid Back painted on the forward cabin bulkhead as well as across the transom facing the dock.

It was after 3:00 when we said goodbye and promised to keep Rose informed of our progress.

Back in the car, Yolanda asked me "What next?"

"I doubt if Doc will be feeling much better by now," I replied.

"That's a given," Yolanda laughed. "Let's pencil that interview for later in the week. Probably should call ahead before we stop by." We both laughed at that.

"Jordan Harbor? We could go look for a boat called Laid Back."

"Maybe save us a trip back up here," Yolanda said looking straight ahead through the windshield. "Let's do it."

CHAPTER TWENTY-FOUR

I started the car and we backtracked in the direction of the coast. On our second pass along the docks, I sighted our quarry. I had almost missed the boat as half of its superstructure had been blown away and the name Laid Back was partially hidden by the canvas draped over the forward cabin.

I parked the Saab a few feet down in front of a pile of sticks that I think had been a bait shop before the storm. Yolanda and I walked back along the wharf to the Laid Back. "Request permission to come aboard," I shouted. "Ahoy, Laid Back, anyone home?"

After a minute or two, a head came up through a hatch on the aft deck. It was a sun-darkened face with a short salt-and-pepper beard and a dark pony tail trailing over one shoulder. Like the Punxsutawney groundhog on a cold spring morning, the head popped up and then was gone, pulling the hatch shut behind him.

"Vince Dominguez?" I called. "We come in peace. I'm trying to prove that your nephew, Johnny, was murdered, to get some justice for him. Can you please come out and talk to me?"

We waited another few minutes in which we heard a shipboard toilet flushing, then the small square in the deck came slowly up again.

"If you're a cop, this is entrapment," came the man's hesitant voice. "There's no marijuana on my boat."

"I'm a *private* cop," I called back. "I'm working for your brother, Jesse."

"Jesse?" he shouted back. "Me and Jesse don't get along. I can't help you." He started to bring the hatch cover back down.

"I thought you liked your nephew Johnny." I said with some urgency in my voice. "Don't you want to help me catch the person who murdered Johnny?"

The hatch cover hesitated, half open, for over a minute then fell back to slam on the deck. The bearded man climbed up onto the deck. He wasn't wearing a shirt or shoes, just a frayed and faded pair of khaki shorts that looked older than my car. The man's eyes were very red.

"So can you talk to me about your nephew Johnny?" I asked.

"You're sure you ain't a cop?" the hippie looking man asked.

"Like I told you," I replied. "I'm a *private* cop. I've got no interest in drugs. I've been hired strictly to find out who killed your nephew and bring them to justice. I don't care if you've got a huge hydroponic garden of grass below deck on your boat... In fact, if you do, I'd be happy to light up with you and share some."

That brought a relaxed chuckle to the man I assumed was Vince Dominguez. "Hey, brother," he laughed. "Welcome aboard. I apologize for being cautious, but a man can't be too careful these days here in Texas. Like, I'd go to Colorado but they don't have an ocean." He laughed again. "A man has to keep his priorities straight." Vince Dominguez brought his right arm back in a welcoming gesture. Yolanda and I walked up the short gang plank to join him on the aft deck of the shrimp boat.

Vince led us forward into the remnants of a cabin. There was a Formica-topped table fastened to the deck and three or four stools scattered around the space, but one side of the cabin wall was missing. He upended two of the fallen stools and motioned us to sit. He righted another for himself and sat facing us.

"So, I heard that Johnny had fallen out of the Ferris wheel at Sea Fair and it was an accident. That's not what happened?"

"Johnny did fall off the ride," I told Vince. "But I don't believe it was an accident. I saw another boy undo his safety harness and give him a push."

Vince scooted back on his stool and thought for a minute. "For real?" he inquired.

"I witnessed it," I replied emphatically.

Vince turned to the console of his boat and dug around in a drawer beside the vessel's wheel. He brought out a zip-lock baggy, opened it and began crumbling bits of organic matter between his fingers. From the pocket of his shorts, he pulled a pack of Zigzag papers. "You want some of this?" he asked. "This conversation is getting a bit heavy for me."

I declined Vince's smoke and waited while he rolled his joint, fired it up and took a hit.

"So you saw my nephew fall off that carnival ride?" he finally asked me.

"I saw him *thrown* from the ride," I told the man. "Tossed like a rag doll by another young man whom all the local people want to dismiss and protect. So, what can you tell me about Johnny? What kind of person was he? Was he the type to take his own life? Or to ask a friend to push him out of a carnival ride one-hundred feet in the air?"

Vince took another long slow hit from his stick of grass. "Johnny was a genius," Vince told us. "I've heard that sometimes genius is very close to crazy... But I can't believe that Johnny would want to kill himself.

"Johnny had so many things planned. He wanted to write a string quartet. He was hoping that his clarinet playing might win him a music scholarship somewhere, maybe North Texas State. And he wanted to compose some music that his girlfriend, Vanna, could dance to. Johnny was way ahead of his time, far beyond his age in years. I don't know about Jesse and Melba, but I was very proud of that boy. He might have been the brightest beacon our family every produced." Vince paused to take another hit from his joint.

"Never had any kids of my own, uh, that I knew about... But I've always been proud of Johnny..." He hung his head, and I could see a tear forming in the man's eye.

"Did you know his friend AJ?" I asked.

"I never met the kid," Vince told us, "but Johnny used to tell me that there was some bully named AJ who was after him a lot, wouldn't give him much peace. Johnny and I would smoke a little reefer and I'd tell him he had to keep a positive attitude, just smile at the boy, be nice to him and drive him crazy until he came around." Then Vince's head tipped down and there was a real tear rolling down his cheek. "I guess it didn't work," he told us.

Yolanda stepped forward and gave the man a hug. "Don't blame yourself," I told him. "This Laudermaelk kid is a pretty twisted piece of work from all we've found. It isn't your fault. We know you loved Johnny and tried to do the best you could for him.

At that, Vince smiled and thanked us as he rolled another joint. We said our goodbyes and thank you's as we stepped off the shrimp boat and walked back to my Saab.

CHAPTER TWENTY-FIVE

We made another pass by Doc Heffernan's place but his car was gone. He must have gone shopping or out to eat something. We'd have to pencil him in for another day.

"Back to Corpus?" I asked Yolanda.

"That sounds like a plan," my partner answered.

"How about a stop at BJs Brewery for a staff meeting on what we have so far?"

"We could sum that up while we drive home," she told me.

"But I refuse to talk shop until I have an IPA in front of me... Or something stronger."

"A hard bargain," my lady told me with a pensive face. "So I guess it'll be BJs then. And I'll require some appetizers as well to get my brain functioning."

After a couple rounds of drinks and a small pizza we headed out for our temporary residence. On the way back to our hotel, we stopped at a market called Specs for a bottle of Scotch. Feeling that we were making progress in spite of the state hijacking all my files, I sprung for a good bottle of Lombard Scotch, a single malt from the Isle of Man.

Back in our hotel room, Yolanda turned on the idiot box while I poured us each a fair measure of the expensive Scotch whiskey. The television was replaying scenes of Rockport and Jordan from the night Nathan struck.

We watched the wind scatter Rusty's patio deck across the neighborhood and water rising along Austin Street, Rockport's historical district. There were crazy television reporters standing in the wind and rain, trying to describe the devastation they were witnessing. For a whole minute we watched a downed power line blowing in the wind, sparking each time it came in contact with a nearby abandoned truck.

"Do we really want to watch this?" I asked Yolanda. She seemed mesmerized by the destruction on the small screen.

Yolanda leaned in toward the hotel's big screen television, shook her head side-to-side as though to clear her thoughts, then turned back to me.

"Sorry, Dave... It's just so, so, ugh, compelling. I just can't believe what I'm witnessing." With that, she felt around the bed for the remote and, finding it, she turned off the TV and sat up straight.

"So, back to our case..." I prompted. "What do you make of the testimonials we've heard today?"

"Well," my partner began, "I've never doubted that Johnny was thrown from that ride, I think the videos we've collected proved that. And, Johnny's relatives all say he was a very smart kid who was aware of the bright future he had. I just don't understand why nobody in authority wants to acknowledge this. Didn't we already go over this at BJs?"

"Ames Laudermaelk seems to be the key to this entire issue," I told her. "We both know he's corrupt. What we need to discover is what hold does he have on so many elected official and law enforcement officers. I know this is Texas, and Texas has a reputation for strange politics, but there has to be something else here we are missing, something that's eluding us. Maybe if I'd been here longer..."

I poured us each another wee dram of the very good Scotch. Yolanda turned the television back on, to watch the damage Nathan had done to the area north of Houston. We listened to reports of how elected officials on the take had allowed developers to build tracts of houses in the flood zone behind more than one flood control dam, just more reassurance that I was right about corrupt officials around this state. Before we knew it, the Scotch bottle was empty and we were drifting off to sleep.

CHAPTER TWENTY-SIX

T he next morning was painful. Yolanda and I were both hung-over and a little nauseous. I'd nearly lost track of time since Nathan had struck. My cell phone told me it was a Thursday morning almost two weeks later. Where had the time gone?

I made a number of calls trying to sort out what was going on with the state cops taking all the files from my office. The Department of Public Safety in Austin said they were unaware of any such order. The governor's office was a total stone wall with live operators switching me into a labyrinth of computer generated menus and, when I'd hit the "0" key to get back to a live human being, the game would start all over again.

By 11:30, I gave up on reaching anyone in the state government who could aid me. With Yolanda's help, I began surfing through anti-Republican blogs. On Facebook, I found a site called "Greg Abbott: Texas-Sized Liar and Nut Case." This web page pretty much told it like it is, although no mention was made of Ames Laudermaelk or his anti Hispanic racial leanings. When I did a Google search for Ames, I got a commercial web page extolling the virtues of the Laudermaelk Agency, LLC, complete with page after page of testimonials from satisfied customers.

I decided if we were to accomplish anything, we would need to drive up to Austin and start confronting people face-to-face.

That is, if we could get through the gatekeepers surrounding our so-called public servants.

Before we left our hotel, I wrote up a brief summary of the harassment I'd suffered at the hands of Ames Laudermaelk and the governor's office. I went back to Facebook and posted my rant on the Greg Abbott: Texas-Sized Liar and Nut Case page. It was probably a foolish idea, destined to cause me more harm than good, but it made me feel better just doing it.

The uniformed ladies manning the desk at the Austin Department of Public Safety office were all smiles and friendly cheer. But that was about as far as it went.

"Do you have an accident report number we can look up?" the woman asked me. "We'll be happy to print out a form for your insurance company."

"It was no accident." I told the smiling twenty-something.

Her face clouded over. "I'm sorry. What kind of incident are you wanting to report?"

"I'm wanting to report one or more of your uniformed DPS men looting my personnel property from my office in Rockport following Hurricane Nathan."

The woman took two steps back, her face registering surprise. "Sir," she said, quite indignantly, "We are here to enforce the law, not to break it."

"Nice bit of rhetoric," I told her, "But one of your uniformed troopers, Ralph Hughes, was looting my office two days ago. The man refused to give me his badge number or the name of his superior officer, but he was violating my business just the same. So who can I talk with to file this complaint?"

The girl appeared flustered. "I don't know how to respond," she told me. "Excuse me while I make some inquiries."

The girl disappeared into the back of the office. I stood there and waited for over an hour, but she never returned. The next person who came to the desk informed me that the DPS office was closing and I should leave.

"We'll be reopening tomorrow at 8:00 am," she told me.

"And what happened to the clerk who was assisting me when I came in?" I asked.

"Well, I understand that Kelly was called to an emergency meeting at the state capitol," she smiled. "I'm sure she'll be back tomorrow morning. I'm going to have to ask you to leave now." As she said it, a uniformed trooper entered from the door behind her, where the clerk she called Kelly had exited an hour before. The man had a tense hand resting on his handgun. He wasn't smiling.

Yolanda and I looked at each other. Putting things off until closing was the oldest ruse in the world. Something here was rotten and these people didn't seem to know who or what they were dealing with. We returned to our car more confident than ever that we could win this case.

When we left the Austin Public Safety barracks, an unmarked car eased out behind us and followed us until we turned off the Interstate to look for some lunch along South Lamar Street. In a residential neighborhood just before we reached Lamar, the car sped up right on our tail, lighting up red and blue warnings from behind the car's grill and windshield. I pulled over onto an unstable grass shoulder and got out while Yolanda turned on the video recorder on her I-Phone.

I got out of my Saab with my driver's license in my hand and stood with my hands out to my side in a non-threatening posture.

The man who emerged from what I'd assumed to be a police vehicle was dressed in blue jeans, a black tee-shirt and a navy watch cap pulled low over his eyes in spite of the Texas heat. As he approached, I saw two other men in similar dress unfolding themselves from the car's rear doors.

The car's driver lunged at me, grabbed my arm and spun me around, throwing his left arm around my throat in a choke hold. One of his accomplices rushed forward to punch me in the gut, then tried to kick my legs out from under me.

Yolanda opened her door and stood behind the Saab aiming her video camera at the unfolding scene. The third man whirled around to face her, pointing a large blue handgun at her face.

"Throw the camera over here," he snarled. "There's nothing here that anyone else would want to see."

Yolanda dropped the camera and watched helplessly as the two goons worked me over thoroughly while their mate kept his arm tight around my throat. When they'd finished with me, one of the helpers stepped over to my car and planted a round-house punch on Yolanda's ear that knocked her to the ground. As they walked back to their car, he ground his heel on Yolanda's camera, shattering it into a hundred small fragments of plastic.

Johnny's So Long at the Fair

Through tearing, hazy eyes, I watched as they got back into their car and drove away. Just before I passed out, I noted that the police type Ford they were driving had no license tag, either front or rear. I knew there wouldn't be much point in reporting the incident.

CHAPTER TWENTY-SEVEN

Back at our hotel, Yolanda dabbed first aid cream on my wounds and fed me a handful of pain killers before she began surfing the web, looking for anything that might connect our pseudo-police contacts with the government in Austin. Nathan shaken! From everything she could find, Texas had no state intelligence agency or secret police. But then by the very title "Secret Police," we had to assume they wouldn't be advertised. I cursed myself for not knowing more about this crazy place where I had decided to semi-retire.

Texas is a red state, very red. I understood that the conservatives were in power, and that misinformation media, like Fox News, kept the population guessing while the wealthy oil people and others would soldier on unimpeded.

After hours of Internet surfing, Yolanda finally looked up with a smile. I was half in the bag from a fresh bottle of single malt Scotch and a handful of Percocet by then.

"The Texas Democratic Party has a special website," she told me. "They're going after the Republican rulers and looking for any kind of evidence they can find of malfeasance."

"How do we get in touch with them?" I asked in a hoarse, creaky voice.

"Well," Yolanda told me, "You can file a report or complaint on their web site. But they also have a physical address in Austin."

"So it's back to Austin again tomorrow?" I asked.

"Looks like our best plan," my lady told me. "Maybe we get another hotel room there as well."

We turned in early that night, after watching a funny British sitcom on BBC America. I'm not a big fan of television, but when you're out-of-it on drugs, pain and booze, and stuck in a hotel room, what can you do?"

Friday found us back in the state capitol, knocking on an ordinary looking office door bearing a baby blue sign with the simple initials TDC. "Texas Democratic Congress," Yolanda told me. "This is the place."

The door was answered by a diminutive lady with granny glasses and dark blond hair pulled back in a bun. She wore faded blue jeans, black shoes with flat heals and a gray cardigan over her white blouse.

Looking at us over the top of her spectacles she asked, "Can I help you?"

"We'd like to discuss a problem that we have with the current Texas administration," Yolanda stated. "May we come in?"

"And you would be?" the small lady asked in a suspicious voice.

"My name is Dave Holman," I told her extending my hand. "I'm a private investigator from Rockport, currently working a case against an Austin lawyer named Ames Laudermaelk. May we sit down?"

The lady's face broke into a sort of smirk. "Another complaint against Ames? Yes, I think you'd better sit down. Just a minute while I find an office where you can speak with someone.

"My name is Amy, but I'm just a volunteer here. Let me get one of our own legal people. You probably know you aren't the first." Yolanda and I turned to stare at each other.

Amy disappeared down a hallway. She returned after about five minutes with a tall African American man in a suit that was probably worth half my pension. His full head of hair was starting to turn white, but his neatly trimmed mustache retained a darker color. His body said that he hadn't missed too many days of working out at a gym somewhere.

"This is Warren Dunbar," she said by way of introduction. "He's our sort of expert on Laudermaelk's indiscretions."

Warren stepped forward shaking my hand and then Yolanda's. "Pleased to meet you both." With his left hand he motioned us down the hallway and into a large office with shelves of legal books on three walls. The fourth wall was a picture window looking out at the state capitol grounds.

When we'd both sunk into a very plush white leather sofa, Warren stated, "So you've had a run-in with Ames Laudermaelk. Tell me about it starting from the beginning." He paused to open a drawer in his desk and pulled out a small cassette machine. "You don't mind if I record this, do you? My memory isn't what it was when I was fresh out of law school."

I said I didn't mind and told Warren Dunbar our story with the tape rolling, beginning with what I assumed to be a murder at the Rockport Sea Fair right up through our harassment by the mysterious officers claiming to be Texas Secret Agents. He could plainly see some of my bruises that lent credence to my story.

Dunbar sat in his high-back office chair, his fingers tented in front of a serious face, listening intently. He never interrupted once. When I'd finished my recitation, he began his questions.

"You're sure it was Laudermaelk's kid?" he asked, lowering his head and focusing his eyes on mine.

"I've collected video from a number of witnesses," I answered. "I've confirmed it was AJ Laudermaelk through a number of sources."

"And the victim was Hispanic? You're sure of that? I have had many complaints that Laudermaelk is prejudiced against Hispanics."

"The victim's family has hired me; they're my clients in this. The Dominguez family are of Mexican descent, but they've been in the Aransas county area since before the Texas revolution. Is that right? When Texas defeated Mexico, anyway."

Dunbar gave a big grin. "I know what you mean," he replied. "This was all Mexico if you go back a few years, so why discriminate now?" He shook his head, "Just more 'white-man' craziness."

We all three laughed at this. Who had the right to draw borders? Weren't we all just one people? I understood this but, apparently, it was too abstract a concept for the average southern US mind.

"And these police officers who stopped you, you couldn't get any badge numbers or car registration tags?"

"I started to record them on my cell phone," Yolanda told the lawyer, "But one of the officers punched me, knocked my phone to the pavement and ground his boot heel down to destroy it.

"They came at us so fast," she told the man," we didn't have a chance to look at badges or bumpers."

"I believe they had black tape over their badges," I told the attorney. "I could see the Texas state logo, but the tape crossed the badge just beneath that hiding any names or numbers. I'm pretty sure there weren't any license plates on their car."

"Typical of these Republican thugs," Dunbar chuckled. "They try to hold the upper hand with all the deception they can muster."

To end the interview, Dunbar asked us to give him all the information on the Dominguez family, their contact information, address and phone numbers.

"I think I know a judge who will be in sympathy with your clients," Dunbar told us as he shook our hands at his office door. "Not in the Aransas County district, but still holding some sway in cases like this. Just give me a week or two and you'll see some major changes in your case."

At this point, I gave Dunbar Miles Boatwright's name, explaining that he had agreed to take our case against Laudermaelk. "He's fairly new to the area," I explained, "so he isn't locked into the local good ol' boy network."

"Good luck with that," Dunbar laughed. "This young man just might have bitten off more than he can chew." Then with a big grin he said, "I'll try and stay in touch with you the best I can, but if you don't hear from me, just keep an eye on what is going on around you. I think you'll see some positive developments."

CHAPTER TWENTY-EIGHT

Right after breakfast Saturday, I called Dr. Heffernan's number. His wife, Jen, answered the phone and told us that the good doctor had sobered up and was feeling much better.

"Keep him at home and sober for an hour," I told her. "I'm on my way up there and I have some questions for Michael. As I think I mentioned before, I'm in the middle of a big case and I'll pay whatever his usual rates are for a profile of my perpetrator."

Yolanda and I arrived at Doc's house in Jordan Beach just over an hour later. Michael still sounded a bit surly when he greeted us, but as soon as I told him I was looking for a psychological profile of the young AJ Laudermaelk, his face broke into a grin.

I explained again how I had watched the Laudermaelk child toss Johnny Dominguez from the top of the Sea Fair Ferris wheel, and how no one in an official capacity that I talked to had wanted to pursue the case, and how I was getting stone-walled at every turn by the local law enforcement community.

"I had read about some kid falling from a carnival ride and getting killed," Doc told me with a serious countenance. "Don't recall the Laudermaelk name being mentioned." I stayed quiet and let him give it some thought. "But then I guess with all the family money, old Ames would do plenty to keep the family name from being a part of it."

"So you know the family then?" I had to ask.

"Know? Yes. But I certainly don't like them or what they stand for around here."

"How much do you know about young AJ?" I asked.

"Well, I've counseled more than one troubled child who'd been bullied by AJ, but I've never had the opportunity to talk to the Laudermaelk kid himself. I don't think the family would want anyone trying to help their son. The stigma of any kind of mental problems and all that, and I'm sure the kid is a deep basket of psychosis." Doc thought for a moment, then continued, "I'd love to get him in here for a session or two."

"So can you give me an analysis of what makes this Laudermaelk kid tick?"

"Not without sitting him down and talking to him," Michael told me. "And it wouldn't be ethical for me to even try without having at least a few sessions with the boy."

"So you're saying you can't help me?" I asked.

The good doctor laughed. "I can offer an *opinion*, for whatever that might be worth, but it would be putting my career and license on the line if I asked you to pay for my *opinion*."

"Okay, so what's your opinion of AJ Laudermaelk," I replied with a grin. "If I can't pay you for it, I'll take you and Jen to a fancy dinner and drinks someplace just as an act of friendship." To get the good doctor started, I told him all about my encounter with the boy and his mother the week before at the Laudermaelk castle on Copano Bay.

Doc Heffernan put his head back, his eyes narrowing to tiny slits. He appeared to ponder this for so long that I thought he might have lost the thread. Finally, he opened his eyes and let them bore into me.

"I'll give you my opinion, but I don't want to be quoted and I won't appear in any court or before any panel with what I have to say. This is strictly a conversation among friends, me speaking as someone who has observed certain behavior patterns in a public figure. Is that understood?"

I nodded vigorously while Yolanda voiced that whatever he told us was strictly between us as individuals and not for public ears.

Doc Heffernan sat back lost in thought for long moments before he spoke again. "My first thought," he told us, his left hand tracing circles in the air by his body, "is the boy is crying out for attention."

He appeared lost in thought for another long stretch of time before he spoke again. "The father, Ames, spends more time in Austin or Houston then he does in Rockport. He certainly isn't what you would call a 'hands-on' father. The mother is involved in so many local charities, I doubt if she's there for AJ when he needs someone to talk with or confide in. AJ has, I assumed, been raised by hired help, nurses and nannies? Who knows?

"Probably Hispanic care givers, or some other under-the-radar immigrants whom Ames has on retainer for slave wages. And yet, Ames is always railing on about how worthless these immigrants are. What is his child to think? Daddy says these people are less than human, but he trusts them to raise his son? How would that make young AJ feel? What does this do for his maturing self-worth?"

"My God," Yolanda whispered beside me. "His own son, inadvertently, told he has no worth."

"And this is reinforced," Michael spoke over her loudly, "by the fact that neither of his parents have any time to spend with him, except of course, when he's excelled in something that will put their own name before the public, their public. Young AJ is craving not just recognition but love from parents who are too busy to acknowledge him. Each attempt is more outrageous than the one before and each designed to get his parents to recognize him, pay him some attention, even negative attention... give him just a little love and acceptance, even if it's all for the wrong reasons."

At that, the room went very quiet. What could we say? It just made too much sense. When I finally spoke I said, "Thank you, Michael. That's pretty much what I needed to know. I don't understand yet how I can use this information in my investigation, but it puts the child's bullying and acting out in a very real perspective. Thanks for making some time for us."

Yolanda and I hung out with Michael and Jen a while longer, making small talk about Hurricane Nathan and the destruction it had caused in both Jordan and Rockport. I reassured them again that I wanted to take them to dinner sometime soon, but the doc laughed and said, "Where is there left where we could get a good meal? All the restaurants here in Jordan are gone. How about we wait until you finish your case and some of the local eateries have a chance to rebuild?"

CHAPTER TWENTY-NINE

The Doc gave us a lot to think about. In more normal times, I'd have returned to my office and discussed all this with the office Scotch bottle. But these weren't normal times. I didn't have a brick and mortar business place right now and no prospects of acquiring one soon. I felt somehow lost. A hotel room had no character and offered little real privacy. Sure, Yolanda shared my office with me, but two people sharing a hotel room just wasn't the same. It was just too open, too public, no corner to get away and think privately. I guess I'd been sitting in the hotel room easy chair contemplating this for some time. Yolanda later told me I had looked almost comatose.

"Dave," she said leaning down to bump her forehead against mine, "You've been sitting there for over three hours with your arms folded across your chest. If your eyes hadn't blinked every now and then I might have assumed that you were dead. What were you thinking about?"

I shook my head as I became conscious of my partner there in front of me. "Thinking?" I offered in a hoarse voice. "I don't remember."

"Dave Homan," she proclaimed, "That's not good. Are you sure you're feeling alright?"

I shook my head to clear the cobwebs. "It's this 'living in a hotel room' thing," I told her. "I can't think straight living in such cramped quarters."

My partner laughed at that. "Dave, this room is half again larger than our apartment was."

"Yeah," I countered, "but it was *our* apartment. It was private and it was familiar, comfortable, you know what I mean?"

Yolanda gave me a funny look, then her face brightened. "Yes," she said with a sudden broad smile. "Yes, I think I know exactly what you mean.

"First thing tomorrow, we're going to Rockport to find some kind of a temporary office that isn't a public property like a hotel."

We cruised around Rockport for most of the next day. So much of the town was in ruin and so many people with stark faces and empty eyes were walking the streets looking for any kind of shelter. There were long lines outside an old, abandoned supermarket where charity groups were offering free hot meals. By two in the afternoon, we realized we weren't about to find anyplace to rent, either for an office or a place to crash.

We headed back toward Corpus Christi. Just before we crossed the bridge over Corpus Christi Bay, we noticed the wide spot in the highway called Portland, Texas, where we'd been breakfasting at the House of Pancakes. Yolanda suggested we get off the highway and have a look around. Portland had some damage from the recent wind and water, but appeared to be in much better shape than Rockport.

On our second pass along the highway frontage road, we found a small storefront next door to the local newspaper with a 'For Lease' sign in the window. Yolanda took down the phone number and called from her mobile phone.

Our call was answered before the first ring had finished. "You have a storefront for lease?" Yolanda asked.

Fifteen minutes later, we were in a tiny real estate office next door to the Portland Good Will store. The real estate agent introduced herself as Prudence Adams.

"You're really interested in that property?" she asked with excited eyes, "Even though the strip mall faces away from the state highway?"

"That's one of the good things about it," I laughed. "I'm a private detective from Rockport and my office there was leveled by the recent hurricane."

"A private detective," she parroted. "And you'll be occupying the office most of the time?"

Yolanda put her hand on the woman's wrist. "Either Dave or I will be there close to twenty-four hours a day."

"Oh." Mrs. Adams cooed, her smile widening. "I have to disclose that we've had a few break-ins around Portland lately, but if you're a detective, that wouldn't bother you."

Then her face lit up fully, like a theater marquee. "In fact, your presence could be a positive force to protect my other renters."

"Yes, that's possible," Yolanda offered with a straight face, "but what kind of rent would you be asking? And what will it cost us to break the lease when our offices are habitable again in Rockport?"

"Ur, um," Prudence Adams stumbled. "Most of my tenants in that center pay a thousand per month…"

She looked into Yolanda's eyes. My partner kept her face very serious, as though weighing the cost against some other location.

"Well," Mrs. Smith began, "As you are going to be kind of providing some security…"

Yolanda and I remained gazing her way with stone faces.

"Well," she began again, "how about six-hundred…"

Yo and I continued our blank stare.

"Okay, six hundred and the first month's free… And we can do month-to-month after the first six months, a very short lease."

I couldn't help myself. My face broke into a grin. Yolanda, still in deadpan, told her, "We'll take it. How soon can we move in?"

"Don't you want me to walk you through the property first?" Mrs. Adams asked.

"Yes, that would be nice," I told her. "Why don't we follow you over there right now?"

CHAPTER THIRTY

The space consisted of two rooms and a toilet. It appeared that the petitioned off space in the rear had been either a boss's office or a place for storage. It really didn't matter much to me which it had been. It could provide a place to sleep apart from our main office or just to get away for a moment of privacy.

There was an old grey desk in the corner of the store front, looking ex-military, along with a similar surplus metal filing cabinet stuck in a corner. "I'll have the former tenant's junk hauled out of here first thing tomorrow," Prudence promised.

"That's okay," I told her, "Don't worry about it." When she shot me an odd look, I told her that my own desk and filing cabinets had been blown away by the recent storm. "I can pay you for this furniture if you like," I told her looking over the top of my sunglasses."

The real estate agent suppressed a giggle. "Don't be silly, it's yours. Would you like my people to mop the floors and dust before you move in?"

"That won't be necessary," Yolanda told her. "I'm sure you have plenty on your desk right now, what with the recent storm and all."

We gave Mrs. Adams a check for two months along with a small sum for security, although the agent said it wouldn't be required. She gave us the keys and thanked us for our business. We now had a space to work from, paid up for three months and into the next year.

On our way out of Portland we stopped at a large sporting goods store to buy a high-end inflatable mattress and two sleeping bags. It was nearly midnight by the time we'd packed everything and checked out of our Corpus Christi hotel. Two in the morning found us setting up our temporary bed in the back room of our new Portland office. We weren't sure about how we'd be able to bathe yet, but there was that small restroom at the back of our new space. At least we could take a bird bath in the morning using the room's small sink. If we were lucky, we'd find a public beach pavilion someplace with showers.

The next morning, after another breakfast at an International House of Pancakes less than a mile from our new office, we called Melba and Jesse Dominguez to let them know where they could find our new headquarters. Then I called Loretta Sanchez with the same information.

"Dave," Loretta warned me, "We've had a bulletin from the capitol police in Austin. They've requested that anyone coming in contact with you should see that you are detained for questioning. They said that if we take you into custody, they'll be here within a matter of hours to take you to Austin for interrogation."

"Now wait just a minute, Lola," I asked. "Can they legally do something like that?"

"I don't know if they can or not, *legally*, but most departments won't want to question such an edict coming directly from the governor."

"Lola," I replied, a bit louder than I had intended.

"Let's just pretend we never had this conversation, Dave," she spit back. "Don't come around the Rockport Police center until I tell you things have calmed down and I will forget that we've had this little talk as well."

"Lola," I cried, but she'd already disconnected our call. I didn't know where to turn from here. I was suddenly working a case all on my own with no official sources I could turn to. It looked like I'd be flying this plane all by myself, but the job had to be done. "Yo," I told my partner, "It's you and me against the world, babe."

"What about Melba's attorney, Miles?" she asked me with a wink. "We may have more on our side than you think, Dave."

CHAPTER THIRTY-ONE

Unsure just where I stood, I made a call to our attorney, Miles Boatwright, for his advice. After I explained the situation, including the roust in Austin by so-called secret policemen and our subsequent meeting with Warren Dunbar at the Texas Democratic Congress, Miles was quiet for over a minute. I was about to inquire if he was still on the line when he let out a long breath of air.

"Quite frankly, I've never heard of anything like this. They certainly couldn't get away with something like you're describing in Massachusetts."

"I don't think anyone in California would try this kind of move either, not in any recent time. Maybe in the nineteen-thirties, if you believe Dashiell Hammett or Raymond Chandler..."

"Well, I'll be looking into this immediately, Dave," the man told me. "And while I'm at it, I'll file a handful of general writs to protect you. I'll get back to you as soon as I have more information, you can be sure of it. Oh, and can you give me a phone number for this Warren Dunbar and the, what was it, Texas Democratic Congress? These sound like people I should know and stay in touch with."

Next, I phoned my clients, to let them know of the new developments in the case. Melba Dominguez answered her phone on the second ring.

"Mr. Holman," she said in a very up-beat and positive voice. "We've got another good man on our team."

I didn't know how to answer this. Maybe I should listen to Mrs. Dominguez before I gave my bad news. She sounded as though her news was much better than mine. "What have you got, Melba?" I asked.

"We've got a *judge* on our side," she crowed. "I just got a call from a secretary in the 197th Federal Court in Brownsville, down on the border. Judge 'Miliano Garcia, a Democrat whose had a number of run-ins with Ames Laudermaelk, heard about our case and he wants to represent us."

I was stunned and silent for a minute. When Melba asked, "You still there, Holman?" I answered that I was.

"I can't believe this," I told her. "I guess I'm still too much of a novice in Texas politics."

Melba laughed. "Mr. Holman, Texas politics is like the weather, stick around a minute and it will change.

"But seriously, you need to get down to Brownsville and talk to Judge Garcia. He says he can legally protect you from the Republicans who are putting a roadblock against your case. He's already filed a motion to get the state people who are after you to back down."

"So we know who these people are?" I asked.

"No," Melba told me, "but talk to 'Miliano, please. I think he's got the answers to all our problems. He's a very smart and dedicated man. He doesn't need to know exactly who is harassing you, he just has to have what he calls 'probable cause' and he can make the governor answer to what's going on."

I had Yolanda take down all the information from Melba and promised to speak with the judge as soon as possible.

When I'd hung up the phone, I asked Yolanda if she might fancy a trip to the Mexican border.

"That's a dangerous place," she answered. "Is this something that's necessary to help Jesse and Melba?"

"We're not going *into* Mexico," I told my partner, "unless we have to. We're supposed to have a face-to-face with a Texas judge who could help us nail Ames Laudermaelk for corruption and possibly the murder of Johnny Dominguez."

"I'll need to get him together with Boatwright, and soon, to see if they could work together?"

Yolanda sat for a long time, staring at her computer screen. "I love the people of Mexico," she told me without turning her head to look at me.

"But I understand that Brownsville is very close to Mexico, the *wrong* part of Mexico."

"I can empathize with your fears," I told Yolanda, "But we must do all we can to bring justice for Johnny Dominguez."

"I understand this, Dave Holman," my partner told me. "Let me make some calls before we make this trip."

Yolanda made a call to Judge Garcia's office. The court secretary who answered told us that 'Miliano Garcia had left instructions that he wanted to meet with me as soon as possible. She mentioned that Warren Dunbar had referred our case to Judge Garcia, which suddenly brought the entire scenario into prospective. The Texas Democratic Congress had acted with remarkable speed. I was so glad that Yolanda had found their website and steered me there.

But as soon as possible turned out to be toward the end of the week, as Garcia had a full court calendar for the following day and other legal obligations on Wednesday.

We made an appointment to meet with the man at 9:00 am Thursday in his chambers at the old courthouse, 1150 East Madison Street in Brownsville, about a mile north of the Mexican border. We decided to drive down the night before and get a room so we'd be rested and fresh for our meeting with the judge.

With that decided I called Miles Boatwright back and invited him to attend our meeting with Judge Garcia. After I gave him the whole story that Melba had relayed, Miles said he'd be delighted. "I'll see you Thursday in Brownsville," he told me as he rang off.

CHAPTER THIRTY-TWO

J udge Garcia was a rotund man with a broad smile, a happy disposition and a twinkle in his eye. I introduced Miles Boatwright to the judge.

"Counselor Boatwright is the Dominguez' attorney of record in this matter," I explained.

"Are you another California man?" Garcia inquired. "Is that how you know Mr. Holman?"

"I'm originally a Bostonian," Miles told the judge. "After law school, I decided I needed to try living somewhere a bit less stayed than Massachusetts. I thought about California, but the cost of living seemed too high, so I chose Corpus Christi… I enjoy sailing so I kind of wanted to be close to salt water."

Judge Garcia's mouth widened into a broad grin, "I'm so glad that some progressive folks like you are coming to Texas," he told me us he extended his hand. "We seriously need to wrest control from these crazy conservatives and evangelical Christians who are ruining our economy and our once friendly state."

Judge Garcia gave us each a firm handshake, using both hands in a reassuring gesture, then he leaned back in his chair.

"Jesse and Melba have told me about the conspiracy they are facing in trying to win justice for their murdered son, and I'm glad that you both have chosen to help them."

"Not so much a matter of choice," I told the man. "I just happened to witness Johnny Dominguez being thrown from that Sea Fair ride. As a human being, I could do no less than strike out for justice. The more the system opposed me, the angrier I became. I just want to see things made right and if I have to fight this with no one to pay me for my services, I'll still continue to stand against this egregious wrong."

"You're a good man, Holman," the judge chuckled. "We don't get many like you around these parts, but when we do, we treasure you folks. Just let me know anything I can do for you. And you also, Counselor Boatwright, my powers are somewhat limited as I have no direct authority in Aransas County, but rest assured I'll go after the Governor, the Lieutenant Governor and the Speaker of the Texas House in every way I can. And I will be issuing orders from my bench to protect your investigation and I truly believe I can make them stick. If you are harassed again by state police, just have someone call my office and things will be cleared up faster than you can say Pancho Villa!" The judge gave another hearty laugh at his statement.

"Are you a Catholic, Holman?" he asked.

I didn't know exactly how to answer. I needed this man's support but lying to get it wouldn't be right.

"I'm more spiritual than religious," I told the judge.

Again, he laughed to himself. "An honest man, you've earned my respect twice over, Dave Holman. I'm a solid Catholic myself, but my faith gives me the courage to respect men like you who see the world differently.

"And you, Boatwright?"

"Actually, I'm kind of a non-practicing Episcopalian, but I keep the faith in my heart."

Go in peace, Dave Holman and Miles Boatwright," the man smiled, "and do what you can to bring justice for the Dominguez family." He handed us each a business card and we all shook hands once more.

CHAPTER THIRTY-THREE

Outside the Judge's office, Yolanda was waiting for us with a couple cold bottles of water. Even though it was late fall, Brownsville was hot, close to ninety degrees. "Have you got some time to discuss the case with me," Miles asked as he twisted the cap off his water.

"I think that would be a good idea," I told the lawyer, "But I don't want to sit on a bench in this hot sun with just a bottle of water. Do you know of any decent brew pubs around this town?"

Boatwright nodded his head in thought. "What was that place? I was down here on vacation for a week some time back... Yeah, I think it's called the Doghouse Pub and Grill. I believe it's right on our way out of town." He pulled a fancy cell phone from the pocket of his grey suit and talked to it as though it were a person. Seeing the look on my face, Yolanda started laughing as Boatwright asked the plastic square directions to the place.

The phone answered back in a clear, distinct voice, giving directions to the bar. Miles nodded his head at the device as though acknowledging instructions from another person. Yolanda punched me lightly on my shoulder commenting, "Dave, you look like you've just seen a flying saucer land. You really have to keep up more on technology."

We followed Miles' white Lexus sedan up Ruben M. Torres Boulevard from the county justice center to Interstate Highway 69-E, where we turned left onto the highway's frontage road. A mile or so up the freeway, we turned left onto a street called Springmart and then into a nondescript parade of shops where we saw the sign for the Doghouse Pub.

The place looked like a typical sports bar upon entering. There were dartboards and a couple pool tables. Behind the bar was a long row of draught taps. As the hour was too early for the lunch crowd, there were only a couple day drinkers at the bar. Miles ordered us all pints of a Houston brewed India Pale Ale and we sat at a small table away from the other customers.

"I know our 'face-to-face' appointment is still a few days away," Miles began, "but as we're here now, how about you give me the background that you have. When we return to the Corpus Christi area, you can get any physical evidence I should have to me."

As our attorney spoke, I could see Yolanda out of the corner of my eye reaching into her oversized leather purse. She drew out her laptop, pushed her beer aside and placed the computer on the narrow tabletop.

"I've got the best of our evidence right her," she told Miles, turning the screen to semi face him. "We have two separate videos shot by spectators at Sea Fair, both showing the boy we've clearly identified as AJ Laudermaelk grabbing our client's son, Johnny Dominguez, and forcing him out of the Ferris wheel's gondola. One of the clips actually follows Dominguez' body as he falls into the ride's machinery."

Yolanda clicked her mouse over an icon of a Ferris wheel and started the video. "I can slow it down so we can go frame by frame. You can also zoom in by clicking the little telescope icon in the lower right hand corner of the screen and then left-clicking the mouse over the area you want to enlarge." Yolanda then pushed the mouse in front of Miles and tipped her head that he should take control and view the episodes.

Miles ran through both videos at normal speed, then went back to view them in greater detail. "You'll notice that Johnny Dominguez isn't exactly cooperating with his assailant," Yolanda pointed out. "In fact, as you can see, he appears to be fighting for his life while the Laudermaelk kid looks like he's laughing."

"This is very disturbing," Miles said softly under his breath as he backed up the film clip once again to closely study the struggle on the carnival ride. "I don't see how anybody could misinterpret this to be anything but murder."

"Unfortunately," I told the lawyer, "nobody in law enforcement wants to watch this video evidence. Their minds are made up that it was an accident and the case is closed."

"And this allegedly guilty party is the son of Ames Laudermaelk, the "Keep Texas White" advocate you mentioned.

"I did my homework on this guy," Miles told us. "He's a pretty sleazy character from all I've read."

"And from one of Aransas County's founding families," I reminded our attorney. "So he has a sort of God-like image in the minds of local conservatives…"

"Not to mention the current administration in Austin," Miles cut in. "Everything I've read says he invested heavily in getting our governor and his cronies elected, probably supporting that embarrassment who's now occupying the White House as well.

"Has Judge Garcia viewed this video? If he hasn't, you should have given him a copy today while we were in his chambers. Garcia needs to see this!"

"I'll email it to his office," Yolanda assured the man. "Our first objective on today's visit was to make sure the governor's 'arrest-on-site' order against Dave got rescinded."

Miles Boatwright glanced at his wristwatch. "I'm pretty sure that's already been accomplished," he chuckled. "Garcia doesn't seem like the kind of guy who just hangs around."

When Miles Boatwright had finished watching the Sea Fair videos, I told him about my visit to Laudermaelk's office, about the man's infatuation with Vlad the Impaler, and about his idea for impaling immigrants and displaying them all along Texas's southern border. We all agreed that the man had to be sick. "But," I told Miles, "from what I'd read about the Laudermaelk-Jordan family, there had been some sort of genetic screw loose for a few generations."

We went over more details of the case into another round of IPAs before Miles looked at his watch and confided that his secretary was probably about to send the state police out looking for him. "I told her I'd be back in the office by two," he confessed, "Which leaves me about twenty minutes to cover one hundred ninety miles, so I'd better be getting on the road. It's been a pleasure finally meeting you both. I'll be in touch in the next few days." With that, he threw a fistful of bills down on the tabletop.

Johnny's So Long at the Fair

As Miles Boatwright rushed out, I could see he was once again talking to his smart phone, probably making excuses to his secretary for his delay.

CHAPTER THIRTY-FOUR

The drive back to Portland seemed to be taking forever. Yolanda was driving and I was riding shotgun, thinking about where my case might go from here. I desperately needed a walk on the beach to clear my head and help me think. That or a few more beers, but neither beer nor beach were close at hand. By the time we reached the petticoats of Corpus Christi, I spoke up.

"Yolanda," I groused, "do you think we could make a brief detour to BJs? My good feeling from this morning's beers is heading south. If I'm going to get any thinking done about this case, I'll need something more to drink… And we probably should have something to eat as well."

Yolanda raised a knuckle to her forehead in a kind of salute and turned east on South Padre Island Drive, towards BJs Brewery. We exited on Everhart Drive and followed the frontage road to the tavern.

We arrived almost at the end of happy hour and took seats at the bar. I ordered an IPA I hadn't tried before, from the Lorelei Brewery right here in Corpus Christi, making a mental note to check them out when I got a little more free time.

About half way through our first round, a man with graying hair and what I always thought of as a beatnik style mustache and goatee sat down one stool to our right. I said, "Good afternoon," and the man replied "good afternoon" back with a wide smile. He ordered an ale from Stone Brewery in San Diego, California, and I complimented the man on his good taste, being very familiar with Stone's IPA as well as their Arrogant Bastard ale.

We talked for awhile about beer, then the conversation somehow turned to mystery writers. I mentioned that I was a Rockport private detective, whipping out one of my business cards. The man answered with a card of his own.

"I'm the District Attorney of San Patricio County," he grinned. "I've worked a few murder cases in my time, though not so many down here. Most of my murder cases were when I was a public defender in Fort Worth.

"I was a commander in the Los Angeles Police Department," I countered, "I'll bet I've worked more murders than you have."

We both laughed at that. "I'll just bet you have," he chuckled. "And very few of mine were true 'who-done-its.' They were mostly domestic arguments that escalated... or impassioned bar room fights."

We both laughed at that. "Domestics are a policeman's worst nightmare," I chuckled. "I'd rather go up against a troop of Arab terrorists than a husband and wife in a serious argument."

"I hear you," the man said. "So are you working a case around here right now?" he asked.

I figured the more locals on my side... "Actually, I'm investigating a murder from the Rockport Sea Fair," I told the man. "One teenager threw another of his school mates off the carnival's Ferris wheel. I've got video evidence to prove my case, but the

Aransas County locals won't touch it. They don't even want to see the evidence."

"I read something about that," my new friend said, "a young man who fell to his death from a carnival ride. The papers all made it sound like an unfortunate accident."

"Believe me," I told my new friend, "It was no accident. My client's son was pushed, actually thrown from the ride, but the kid who pushed him is AJ Laudermaelk."

"Uh oh," the DA from the next county said, "Laudermaelk, as in 'Jordan-Laudermaelk, the father of Aransas County? I can see the problem you're facing."

"Yeah," I told my new friend, "That's what I'm up against. I've got a smart young Harvard law attorney on my side and a Hispanic judge from down in the valley, but I'm still fighting an uphill battle."

The man thought for a minute, then replied, "I'll have to say there's no love lost between old Rockport money and San Patricio County. I'd love to get something to hold over those stuck-up folks. Let's stay in touch, Dave Holman. Do you like home brewed beer? I brew some pretty hoppy ales of my own. Maybe you could come over some time to sample some of my ale and we'll see how I might be able to help with your case."

I filed the man's information away. He could come in handy somewhere down the road, if not in the case, possibly one in the future.

CHAPTER THIRTY-FIVE

R ockport Beach remained closed. The famous Rockport Blue Crab statue, what was left of it, rested in shallow water just off the sand. The palm leaf cabanas were strewn across the area in ruin, and debris from all along the coast washed up to clog the crescent of shoreline that marked our tourist site. And much of our sand had been washed out to sea.

I ventured out to take my first post Nathan beach walk but was stopped by a security guard at the park entrance. "The beach is closed until further notice," he told me. "The area is unsafe and the pavilions are unstable. Also, there are nails and screws all over the road and we've had reports of rattlesnakes washing up on the shore."

"I'll take my chances," I told the man, but he wasn't buying it.

"We'll get some crews out here by the weekend," he told me with a darkly clouded face. "You could check back on Monday, but I ain't promising anything."

I thought about sneaking around to the breakwater where a couple old cowboys were fishing. I could climb down the rocks and wade in to the sand, but from the edge of the rocks I could see part of a house and some large boards that looked like they came from a broken-up dock floating close to the shore. I decided to try North Beach in Corpus Christi instead. It was close to Portland and our temporary digs. Also, there wasn't a gate there that could lock me out.

It was past noon when I slotted the Saab into a space in the Burleson Beach Park at the end of Breaker Avenue on Corpus Christi's North Beach. Down the sand to my right, I could see the World War II aircraft carrier Lexington, and I decided to start my trek in that direction.

As I walked, I could see condos and hotels along the beach that had some hurricane damage. Crews were already pulling ruined wall board out of a large Ramada Inn. The Lexington, in the distance, brought back memories of Viet Nam, when a similar craft, the USS Princeton, had come close to shore to rescue my crew of amphibious Coast Guardsmen.

The beach was mostly deserted, but there were a few small groups barbequing hot dogs and burgers, drinking from cans of beer and looking out to sea.

Near a restaurant called Fajitaville, I saw where someone had created a very realistic sand sculpture of a woman. I stopped to give it a closer look, marveling at how realistic this bit of art appeared. It looked like a woman lying on her back, spread eagle, with her arms out like the Leonardo DiVinci man. I continued on down the strand. Coming even with the fantail of the Lexington, I turned around to head back.

Nearing Fajitaville, I heard a horrendous scream and saw a young man standing, his whole body shaking, with a look of total terror. I ran up the berm to see if I could help. By then, the man had lost the contents of his stomach onto the sand near the sculpture.

Following the young teen's gaze, I saw where he had kicked at the sand sculpture of a woman only to expose some very pale and real human flesh. Her newly exposed and macabre white head gave up an empty stare through vacant eyes.

It appeared as though someone had laid the body out on the sand and then smoothed a thin layer of sand over her dead flesh. How long it had been there was anyone's guess.

The Corpus Christi police arrived within minutes. There were two black and whites on either side of my Saab in the parking lot. The uniforms who arrived in those units were only interested in cordoning off the crime scene. I introduced myself and one of the officers said he remembered me from a few years back when a dead African national had turned up in a downtown Corpus alley.

We waited another twenty minutes for the coroner and some crime scene investigators to arrive. By the end of an hour, they had dug out the body of a young girl. The detective who followed them estimated her age at around fifteen and speculated that she'd had sex with someone within the past twenty-four hours.

"There're no bruises and no blood," the officer told me. "This could be a troubling case. We'll have to wait until the autopsy boys have a look at her."

Another plain-clothes man who'd been checking out the scene cleared his throat.

"Ah, chief?" he said without looking up from the corpse, "There appears to be some vomit around her chin."

At that, both the detective I'd been talking with and one of the crime scene techs leaned down for a closer look at our little dead girl.

Skoot Larson

"Choked on her own vomit," the crime scene guy whispered.

"Let's not draw any conclusions until we've had a thorough investigation into the facts," the plain clothes man scolded, but with my own eyes I could see the foul liquid on her lips. I could also smell cheap booze when I leaned in closer.

CHAPTER THIRTY-SIX

I arrived home late to find Yolanda at her desk surfing the Internet. "I found a dead girl on North Beach in Corpus," I told her.

"I know all about that, Dave," she replied without looking away from her screen. "It's been all over the news."

"That was pretty fast," I told her. "Have they identified her?"

"More than that, Dave, her picture has gone viral on Facebook…"

"What, some girl found hours ago has already made it to Facebook?"

Yolanda gave a hollow laugh. "Not just 'some girl,' Dave, the photo on Facebook is of her dancing with our own local Congressman, Brent Holloway, and she isn't exactly dressed."

"Brent Holloway?" I parroted. "The guy who always says he's standing up for veterans? And what do you mean 'isn't exactly dressed?'"

"Brent Holloway, one and the same," Yolanda answered with a wink. "The congressman says he *did* dance with her at a fund-raising party Saturday night, a pajama party he called it, and yes, she wasn't wearing any clothes, but he claims that he was unaware that she was fifteen years old. She was only wearing a crimson thong. He's blaming his security people for not checking the ages of people attending the bash at the door."

"The Corpus police said the victim they found had recently had sex..."

"Then they'd better get a sample of Holloway's DNA," she cut me off.

"So, have you done any background on Holloway?" I had to inquire.

"Arsehole buddies with Ames Laudermaelk," my partner fired back. "In fact, we've had reports the Ames attended that party in Corpus although he claims he was at his home in Austin. I'm going to hack into the state's computer system, if you don't mind, to look for proof that Ames attended the party."

"Have they said who the girl is?" I asked.

"Now there is another interesting study," Yolanda replied, "The girl's name in Candace Keene. She's a straight 'A' student at Rockport-Jordan High School, but it's rumored that she's also a serious party girl. The few from Senator Holloway's fundraiser that would talk to the Corpus cops said they knew her as Candy Keene. Oh, and she was also close friend of young AJ Laudermaelk."

Just after Yolanda had mentioned AJ Laudermaelk, The photo on Facebook of Candace Keene popped up at the head of the postings with an attached comment purporting to be from young AJ.

"My father is responsible," he wrote. "He's an animal, and none of my friends are safe around him. He's always trying to seduce any girl I might bring home. Make no mistake; Ames Laudermaelk killed my friend Candy."

There were a few other replies, a few defending both Laudermaelk and Congressman Holloway, but many more siding with AJ. At the end of the stream was another comment from AJ. "Okay, I killed Candy. I held her nose until she stopped breathing. What could I do? She'd had sex with both Brent and my father, but she didn't want to have sex with me, the bitch."

Yolanda turned towards me, her face asking, could this be true? I didn't have an answer. Doc Heffernan had said the boy was reaching out for attention, from anywhere he could find it as he wasn't getting any recognition at home. Would he create a lie this big in order to be noticed? Or would he go so far as to commit a murder?

While we were pondering this dilemma, the phone rang. It was Lola Sanchez.

"You've seen the statement on Facebook?" she asked. "What do you think; could AJ be telling the truth?"

"He could be," I answered, "But I'd like to know a lot more about what happened last night before I'd try to convict him. Could his father be sacrificing him? Or is he feeling guilty about something else he might have done, seeking punishment for that burden of guilt?"

"I'd really like to meet with you Dave. We need to compare notes and discuss this situation, but you're still on that arrest-on-sight order from Austin."

"Better check with your chief, Lola," I told her. "A judge down in the valley filed papers to declare that arrest order null and void a couple days ago. If the rescind order hasn't gone out yet, then my attorney is going to have the governor's balls on a silver platter, not to mention Sam Smith, the DA of San Patricio County.

"Besides, I spent much of the day with the Corpus cops and no one mentioned any arrest order," I told her with a grin she could probably sense right through the phone.

"Maybe the state made a bigger thing of it in Rockport because this is your home town."

"Or maybe the Corpus Christi guys just have a better bullshit detector..." I started to say.

"Dave Holman, try to be civil here. All I know is what we're given at roll call each shift and they've been saying to be on the lookout for you over the past three days."

"Alright, alright," I told her. "How about we meet at the Taco Bell in Portland..." Before Lola answered, I thought for another moment. "Better yet, just beyond the Taco Bell. Off Wildcat Drive and the freeway is a little used bookstore, Book's Ink I believe it's called. Come in mufti and we can sit and talk hidden back among the stacks of old books."

"Mufti?" she giggled, "mufti?"

"Civvies," I shouted back into my phone. "Civilian clothes, no uniform."

"Okay Dave," Lola laughed out loud. "I know 'mufti,' it's just that I hadn't heard anyone say that since I was a teenager watching public television. Give me an hour, I'll be there."

CHAPTER THIRTY-SEVEN

D anny Lazlo arrived at Book's Ink with Lola, but the lady detective assured me that it was cool, Ray was on our side.

"How you doin', Dave," he grinned. "Looks like you survived Nathan without too much hardship."

"Are you kidding?" I asked incredulously.

"Just making conversation," he chuckled. "We all got hit hard. I'm livin' in a burned out old RV I managed to drag onto my property. My son and daughter think it's an adventure, but the wife hates it. She keeps threatening to take the kids to her mother's in Marfa." His grin broadened some. "Oh, if only."

"Enough boy talk," Lola said to silence us. "We've got a serious situation on our hands here." Then looking directly at me, she added, "We've traced that Facebook post of our vic dancing with Congressman Holloway to one of the computers in Ames Laudermaelk's Rockport office, except that no one's been in that office over the past week. We sent a patrol by and the place is locked up solid with all the alarms set. All of Ames' local staff have alibis for the past thirty-six hours, so there should have been no one in that space."

"And the postings from AJ claiming Ames is responsible and none of his friends are safe?"

"We've traced *those* to AJ's cell phone, for what it's worth."

"What do you mean, 'for what it's worth'?" I asked her.

"'Cause AJ's phone dropped off the face of the earth right after we made the connection," Lazlo chuckled. "One minute it was there, the next minute it's gone into deep outer space."

"Not just the phone," Lola added. "Young AJ is missing as well. Law enforcement all over south west Texas are looking for him so we can question him about his claim that he killed Candy Keene. He's nowhere to be found. We're thinking that if he's in hiding, he might have been smart enough to pull the battery out of his phone..."

"Or he just smashed the thing against a rock," Danny added. "Crazy kids today."

"We've sent guys out to check with his mother, Agnetta," Lola continued, "but she was very drunk and when we asked about AJ, she became hysterical, screaming that she knew he had been beaten and killed by his father.

"After she calmed down a bit, we managed to get the names of some of AJ's friends out of her, but the last I heard we haven't had much luck locating any of them. Agnetta only knew first names for most of them, and had no phone numbers or addresses for any of the people AJ knew. When I reminded her that some of AJ's colleagues were sons and daughters of her own friends, she simply burst into tears wailing that she didn't have any friends, that Ames wouldn't allow her to have friends." After that, no one spoke for a few minutes. Agnetta Laudermaelk had given us a lot to think about.

Jennifer, the owner of Book's Ink, poked her head back into our meeting during our silence. "Could I bring anyone some coffee or pastry?" she asked.

Jennifer is a very well read Jamaican lady who earned her citizenship serving in the US Navy. She used her military retirement to open Book's Ink, which was now her life, along with a passion for playing Scrabble. "It's on the house," she assured us.

Danny immediately said he wanted a black coffee with lots of sugar and asked what kind of cookies she had. Lola hesitantly agreed that she would like a coffee as well, but without the sugar. I just nodded. Yolanda and I were regular customers of the shop as we both shared a love of good 'who-done-its' and Jennifer already knew how I liked my coffee.

After Jennifer had brought our refreshments, Danny asked rhetorically where a spoiled rich kid with an overbearing father and a spineless mother might be hiding. "You think the kid might have fled to his dad's place in Mexico? After all, he just as good as confessed to one capitol murder."

"Has he really confessed?" Lola pondered, "Or is he maybe covering for his father out of some kind of false family loyalty? Or he may be protecting some other kid who did the killing to buy a friendship. We know he doesn't have many real friends. What lengths would he go to in order to obtain a buddy or companion, even a twisted, criminal companion?"

Again, we lapsed into silence, concentrating on sipping our doses of caffeine until Lola broke the silence with, "I don't like where this scenario is going."

We kicked some more ideas around the table. Could one of Ames' people be trying to frame AJ to save his own boss? Or could this whole thing be a smokescreen to take our focus off Ames Laudermaelk.

When our coffee cups were as empty as our list of clues, we decided to call it a day.

CHAPTER THIRTY-EIGHT

With no good answers, Lola and Danny headed back to Rockport while I headed in the opposite direction, crossing the bay bridge back to Corpus Christi. I noted by the Saab's dashboard clock that it was after 5:00 pm, so I phoned Yolanda and asked if she could meet at the Rebel Toad Brewery.

"Wouldn't you rather meet at a restaurant, Dave? Where we could get some dinner?"

I thought about that for half a minute, then answered, "Right now I need something cold to drink. My mind is too twisted up to eat. Maybe after we have a few pints and you help talk me through all this weirdness, I'll get my appetite back. So, Rebel Toad?"

"Okay, sure Dave," my partner answered in a hesitant voice. "I can be there in maybe twenty minutes."

"That works," I told her. "If I get there before you, I'll order you a pint and wait."

Traffic on the bridge was light and I arrived on the old waterfront in less than ten minutes. I circled the block around the brewery a few times and finally found a parking place on John Sartain Street a block away. I walked to Rebel Toad and was just finishing my first pint when Yolanda walked in. She gave me a hug and I pushed her pint glass of ale down the bar toward her. We both took long pulls of our beverages then sat in silence for a minute or two.

"Dave," she began. I shook my head 'no' to ask for a little more silence. I needed to let the alcohol settle in my brain for a few minutes before I could get my thoughts all in line and present them to my partner.

When my glass was nearly empty, I turned to Yolanda and told her about my discussion with Lola and Danny. I also mentioned that Lola had informed me that they'd told the troops at roll call that I was still on the 'arrest-on-sight' list, asking for my partner's take on that.

Yolanda gave it a moment's thought, then said, "Laudermaelk has someone working for him inside the Rockport Police Department?"

"That would be my take on it," I replied, "but who could it be?"

"Somebody pretty high up," my partner gave me with a pensive look. "Not one of the rank and file... But I wouldn't think it could be the chief. Maybe someone who handles messages in and out of the department, someone the chief trusts."

"Yeah, that's what I was thinking," I told her. "But, unfortunately, I mostly deal with the department's foot soldiers, not the high brass. I've dealt with the chief of police and the county sheriff, but I've seldom more than shook hands with their lieutenants."

"And right now?" my partner asked.

"Right now I may be suffering for not engaging in more hand-shaking and back-slapping," I told her. "I should have started that way back at Roger Alper's funeral, when he was shot and I was new to this area."

Just after I had arrived in Rockport, Officer Alpers had been gunned down at a traffic stop with no witnesses. I'd used my former big-city experience and connections to find his killer, for which the Rockport Police had been grateful, but I'd mainly worked with the cops on the street, having an occasional meeting with their chief. I'd had little to do with the middle management guys.

At least Lola and Danny were on my side. I would stay in communication with these two friends. If I had to deal with any of their superiors, I just hoped that my friends would pave the way and stand up for me in the crunch.

CHAPTER THIRTY-NINE

The next day, I decided to drive out to the Laudermaelk castle/ mansion to have another talk of my own with Agnetta. She might be harboring AJ, protecting him from either Ames III or from law enforcement. Or AJ could just be hiding out there and his mother, drunk so much of the time, knows nothing about the dead girl or the party her husband had attended.

Once again, I couldn't believe the utter devastation I encountered driving west through the Copano Bay area. Double wide manufactured homes lay tilted, half off their blocks, stilt homes had pan-caked into piles of rubble and regular ranch-style homes were reduced to stacks of stucco and two-by-fours. Some of the houses still semi-standing bore raw plywood squares with "Do Not Enter – black mold" written in spray paint.

At the end of Old Salt Lake Road, I could see the Laudermaelk place off to my left. Stone fortress that it was, the castle was still standing, although one of the crenulated towers had been blown down by the hurricane and now rested a few yards out on its side in the shallow water of Salt Lake. I couldn't see or hear any of the peacocks that had lived on the property. Maybe they had flown away in the face of the hurricane.

I pulled up near the entrance and noticed that there were huge gaps in the walkway of the bridge to the front door where planks had been ripped out and tossed into the moat below. One large 'gator was sleeping at the far end of the parking area. As I got out of the Saab, the reptile opened one sleepy eye and glanced my way, yawned, then laid his head back down on the gravel. I stepped gingerly across to the front portal and gave the doorbell pull a hard yank.

I pulled the cord two or three more times and was about ready to give up and return to my car when I finally heard uneven footfalls behind the door. It was opened slowly by a wraith-like figure that I hardly recognized as Agnetta Laudermaelk.

She wore a torn and disheveled old cocktail dress, high heel shoes with one of the spike heels twisted sidewise, causing her ankle to buckle over when she walked, and on her face she sported oversized sun glasses. Her upper arms bore yellowing purple bruises and her lip was bleeding on one side. The two small black dogs appeared to be asleep in the corner of a long white leather sofa.

"Come in, pretty man," she said, with an attempt at a smile that appeared to cause her pain. She turned on her heel and headed for the bar with a serious limp. "What do you drink?" she hiccoughed, "I don't seem to remember... And I don't recall your name either, sorry." She laughed. "My memory isn't real good lately..."

"Is AJ at home," I asked her back as she turned to face the bar. "I need to talk with him."

She turned back towards me with a look of confusion, "AJ?" When she turned I could see just how bad off the woman was. "What happened to you, Agnetta?" I asked with real concern.

"Oh... I think I fell down the stairs," she replied, looking at me over the top of her sunglasses. When the cheaters slid down her nose they revealed bruises right across her nose connecting both eyes. Her right eye was nearly swollen shut.

I stepped closer for a good look and placed a hand on her shoulder. "Did your husband do this to you?" I asked.

She shook my hand off. "No, I told you, I fell down the stairs." Then she gave a kind of combination laugh and sob, "Three or four times." She whispered to herself, then shook her head and her sob turned into a giggle. "So what are you drinking? We've got gin an' vo'ka, maybe some bran'y here someplace. You're not a whiskey drinker, are you?" She turned away to dig among the bottles that lined the counter, leaning heavily against the bar. Agnetta finally settled on a gin bottle and poured some clear liquid into her glass. She then spun around and started back toward me, but her left knee gave way over her broken heel and she pitched forward onto her face after two steps, gin and broken glass flying everywhere.

I knelt down to assist her. The drunken woman grabbed my knees and tried to push herself off the floor. I gave her a hand to bring her upright and ended up with her standing pressed against my body. "Have we gone to bed yet, Honey?" she asked with a painful wink of her good eye.

I managed to turn her over and get my hands under her armpits. I dragged her on her heels over the carpet to the white leather sofa where I unceremoniously dumped her back against the cushions.

"Mrs. Laudermaelk," I said, loudly and clearly. "Someone has beaten you severely. I think I need to call an ambulance for you right now. You belong in a hospital. Now tell me, did you have an intruder here or was it your husband? Just give me a simple, truthful answer." She turned her head away and began to cry.

I fished my cell phone from my pocket and started to punch in 911. Agnetta immediately pushed off from the couch and threw her arms around my neck, leaning heavily on me. "Oh please, no." she wailed. "You can't call an ambulance. Ames will kill me, for real. This is a private *family* matter." At her shout, the two schipperkes leaped from the couch and started barking at me.

I brushed Agnetta aside as the emergency operator answered and I rattled off the situation. When the 911 lady asked for an address, I didn't know exactly what to say. "I'm just left off the end of Old Salt Lake Road," I told the woman as Agnetta threw her head back in a howl. The two black dogs howled along with her.

"No, no. Ames swore he'd kill me if I ever shared any personal family business."

Through the phone line, I heard the operator laugh. "You must be at Ames Laudermaelk's place. Can I speak to Ames?"

"Ames isn't here," I answered, "but his wife has been severely beaten. She needs to get to an emergency room ASAP."

Then another voice came on the phone from emergency response. "This is Mel Simpkins, I'm the shift supervisor. To whom am I speaking?"

"My name is Dave Holman," I told him. "I'm a private investigator. I just happened to discover Agnetta Laudermaelk here and she's in rough shape. She needs to get to an emergency room right now."

"I'm sorry, Mr. Holman, but Mr. Laudermaelk has left instructions that his wife is a terrible hypochondriac, and we shouldn't waste our time answering her calls..."

"You listen to me and listen good, Mel Simpkins. You send an ambulance as fast as you can get your fat ass to your desk or you will be up on charges for dereliction of duty and possible criminal negligence, do you hear me?"

"Have you spoken with the sheriff?" he asked.

"I *will* be speaking to the sheriff if I don't have an ambulance here in twenty minutes," I told him. "And I'll be speaking with the Rockport chief and all the area media as well, so get on it!" At that, I slammed down the phone.

While we waited for the EMTs, I told Mrs. Laudermaelk that I would see that she was protected from her husband.

"But how can I live without him?" she asked in a panicky voice. "He'll divorce me and leave me penniless. You don't understand, sir, he owns me. He's a lawyer and he's always said that I can't testify against him, that I'll be the one going to jail. He knows all the laws in Texas."

"That's bullshit, Mrs. Laudermaelk." I told her. "Nobody can *own* another human being. And nobody has the right to abuse another human being.

"Right now, your husband is being investigated on several capital charges and may end up going to prison himself. A Texas divorce court will most likely award you a good portion of Ames' wealth. Trust me, you'll do just fine."

At that, two white-coated men pushed a gurney through the door, with the two dogs at their heels, and took charge of Agnetta Laudermaelk. When they had her in the ambulance, I chased the two schipperke dogs back inside, pulled the castle door shut and checked that it was locked. From my car, I called animal control to get someone to come and rescue the two puppies.

CHAPTER FORTY

From the Laudermaelk castle, I returned to Corpus Christi. I picked up Yolanda and we stopped for a drink at a place called the Seafood Station Brewery near Heritage Park. We were on our second round of the establishment's own locally brewed IPA when Yolanda punched my shoulder and nodded toward the television screen over the bar. I looked up to see a split screen. On one side was an old stock photo of young AJ and on the right of him a black and white school yearbook picture of his girlfriend, Miranda.

The volume was turned down, but the closed captioning trailed slowly beneath their likenesses.

"...body was found in the living room of the Laudermaelk home on Old Salt Lake Drive in Copano Bay by one of the household's staff. Miranda Watkins was rushed to the Code 3 Emergency Room in Rockport where she was pronounced dead on arrival from an overdose of oxycodone and alcohol. Paramedics attempting to revive the young woman found a suicide note tucked in her bra. Rockport Police declined to comment on the note at this time."

The screen cut to the view of the salt lake from the Eyewitness News Tele-copter, while a voice pleaded that we "stay tuned for more information."

I cursed myself for not taking the time to check out the rest of the house while I was there rescuing Agnetta Laudermaelk. The girl must have been there all the time, maybe in the next room. I quickly dug out my cell phone and called Loretta Sanchez at the Rockport Police Station. "So Dave Holman, are you calling to gloat over this," she answered in a shaky voice. I silently cursed caller ID on telephones. Then out loud, I said, "Strictly in confidence, does anyone care to share the contents of Miranda's suicide note?"

"Officially, no," she told me, then in a lowered voice, almost a whisper she added. "Jesus, there isn't even anyplace left where we can secretly meet for coffee in what's left of this town. How about you drive out to the Salt Water Pool on Rockport Beach? Park by the one remaining picnic cabana that Nathan didn't flatten and I'll be there as soon as I can get away? Hopefully within the hour."

"How soon, realistically?" I questioned.

"I can't say, Holman. As soon as I can, got to go." And she hung up.

I dropped Yolanda back at our hotel and headed up Highway 181 toward Rockport. Getting off the freeway, I stopped at the local McDonald's and bought two large coffees to go, then cruised out along Rockport Beach to the far east end.

Our two Beach Pavilion bath houses stood gaping, the wind from the hurricane having torn off the outer walls and much of the roof. Just east of the second pavilion, across the Salt Water Pool, I had a great view of Key Allegro. I could see where one house had slid into Little Bay and a few others showed major damage. I took the McDonald's bag out to the small table overlooking the channel to wait for Lola Sanchez.

Lola showed up about fifteen minutes after I arrived. She was driving her own personal vehicle and when she stepped out, she was wearing a green Rockport High School Pirates hoody that concealed her face.

"The girl was pregnant," she said as she approached me. Lola had tears in her eyes.

"And good afternoon to you, too," I replied with a small smile. "I hate to say I told you so." I held a paper cup of coffee out to her.

"Don't, Dave. Please don't."

"All of you in the department wanted to defend this Laudermaelk kid…"

"It wasn't me, Dave, honestly." Lola shook her head then buried it in her hands. "It's Aransas County politics.

"I like my job. I didn't want to say anything to jeopardize it. I'm sorry, Dave! I feel like shit and I don't need you to rub it in."

"Lola." I put my arm around her shoulder, but she twisted away and shook it off, taking a step back from me.

"The note she left…" Lola's whole body shivered. I gave the lady detective her space while she pulled herself together. Her body went through a couple more spasms and she began to cry. I handed her my pocket handkerchief and waited.

After another minute, Lola blew her nose, squared her shoulders and looked at me. "Miranda's note said she was pregnant but she wasn't sure if the baby was AJ's child or his father's." Tears filled her eyes again. "That poor girl!"

"Lola," I whispered, offering my arms once more to give her a hug.

"Her note said that Ames Laudermaelk raped her repeatedly. He forced her to have sex with him. Even in front of young AJ. He told his son that sharing a woman was part of becoming a real Texas man, a *Laudermaelk* man." With that, her face clouded over and tears filled her eyes once more. Between spasms of crying, Lola managed to cough out, "It's so terrible I can't even believe. What kind of animal..." She then broke down in tears once more and folded herself into my arms.

CHAPTER FORTY-ONE

Loretta Sanchez' breathing was almost back to normal when her cell phone chimed. She looked up at me and I nodded that she should answer the call. "Speaker phone," I mouthed to her.

"Officer Sanchez?" came the voice from her I-Phone, "We need every available officer to report to Rockport Jordan High School immediately. We have reports of a student armed with an assault rifle in Martha Luigi Auditorium. We have one confirmed dead and three wounded, according to reports from students on their cell phones. Make sure you have your vest on."

"The high school?" she replied with an incredulous face. "Here, in Rockport?"

"Just get down here!" the voice on her mobile shouted, then hung up.

"Dave?" The look Lola gave me was pitiful. It said, 'how could this be happening here?'

I held her tighter for a second, then said, "We'd better get a move on."

"Do you have a vest?" Lola asked me.

"I don't need one," I told her. "We're dealing with a confused kid here. I think I'll be alright."

Lola gave me a skeptical look, and then said, "Ride with me Dave. No need to bring another vehicle into this."

We arrived at the high school campus within minutes, driving up Omohundro Street from the beach. The school parking lot along Enterprise Boulevard was filled with police and sheriff's units, all with their blue and red lights rotating in the bright afternoon sun. There were officers with rifles kneeling behind the doors of their vehicles, and a few senior men walking gingerly around the perimeter of the lot. Across the street, a large knot of students paced nervously behind saw-horse style barricades, keeping a close eye on their school buildings.

I told Lola to just bring us across Enterprise and park as close to the auditorium's doors as she could.

"Dave?" she questioned.

"I've got this in hand," I replied.

As we got close, a cop I couldn't recognize because of his riot gear, blocked our path to wave us away. He wasn't in the least phased by Sanchez's police ID.

Seconds later, Lola's radio lit up. "Sanchez, are you crazy? What the fuck are you doing?"

"Don't answer," I told her. "Drive around by the back of the Dairy Queen and let me out. I'm betting there's a rear entrance to the auditorium."

"Yes, there is, but why would you go in there?"

"We're dealing with a sick kid here," I reminded Lola again. "Killing him won't solve anything. I'm going in to talk with AJ.

Maybe, just maybe, I can save his life before a bunch of trigger-happy cowboys blow him away."

The stage door at the rear of the building was locked, but it was a simple task to slip a credit card into the door frame and ease the tongue of the lock back. Thankfully, the door didn't give a creak or a clank when I forced it open. I took off my shoes and set them beside the door. In stocking feet I proceeded around the back of the stage to a curtain that was lowered over the proscenium. I found a set of steps on the left side of the area that led through an opening into the full theater.

I glanced out to see a half dozen people, both teachers and students, cowering in the middle rows of the large hall. One or two noticed my entrance. I prayed that they wouldn't give me away.

At the bottom of the steps I turned my head to see AJ Laudermaelk standing behind a sort of speaker's podium, one rifle slung over his shoulder, another resting on the lectern before him. His shoulders seemed very tense as his eyes swept the room before him. When his eyes would touch a member of the crowd, that person would shrink back as though AJ's look burned them. AJ held his audience in a fear of death. He knew he controlled all the power.

I sensed that someone had entered the backstage door behind me. Lola, I hoped. I didn't need any wanna-be cop hero spoiling my plan.

I cleared my throat loudly to get AJ's attention. He spun in my direction, bringing his rifle up to aim at my chest.

"I'm ready to kill you, mister," he barked in a hoarse voice. "I'm ready to kill anyone from my father's world."

"I'm not from your father's world," I told him in a calm voice, showing more confidence then I really felt. "In fact, I hate your father's world. He was trying to destroy my life and everything I believe in."

With this, I could see young AJ's tight jaw loosening somewhat.

"You're lying," he shouted in a hesitant voice, setting his jaw firmly once more. "You're one of the cops who he's bought and paid for. You're just another corrupt piece of shit doing my dad's bidding."

"Listen to me, AJ," I shouted, "And listen good. My name is Dave Holman. I used to be a cop, out in California. I have never been a Texas cop and I've never worked for your father. In fact, your father has been trying to destroy me. I'm on your side, you and Miranda."

"Miranda's dead," he sobbed loudly, throwing his head back. "She had to kill herself thanks to my father. She was the only person who ever really loved me. My mom was so terrified of my father, she couldn't love anyone. So now I'm going to join her… Miranda." The boy tried to turn the assault rifle in his hands around to aim at his own head, but when the gun was pointed at him, he couldn't quite reach the trigger with his fingers.

He was silent for three or four minutes. The whole room was quiet except for AJ's sobbing. So quiet we could hear someone in the lobby, trying to force their way into the auditorium.

"AJ?" I called out in the silence. "You've got a good life ahead of you. You can *fight* against people like your father. You can make the world a better place."

With the gun still loosely pointed towards himself, AJ cried out, "Did you know my father? I don't think you did! My father was a hypocrite. I don't want to be part of a world like my father's world. I hate my father. He drove Miranda to kill herself."

As AJ spoke, I could see police in SWAT gear entering at the back of the large room and lining up across the rearmost rows of seats. I held up my hand for them not to interfere, not to shoot before I had a chance to turn this young man around.

"I don't ever want to be like my father," he screamed. "I don't want to be an attorney. All my father's attorney friends are corrupt, hateful men."

"I can understand that," I told AJ in a soft, caring tone. "And you don't have to be. You can be anything you want. You can't bring Miranda back, but you can fight for a cause, for justice. You can make sure that Miranda is remembered, that she didn't die in vain.

"If you'll just put your guns down on the stage floor and step away from them."

As I said this, I noticed at least three rifles in the back row of the auditorium tracking young AJ.

"There are some policemen in the back aiming their guns at us," I shouted. "Please, put your guns down as well, as soon as AJ sets his weapons down and steps away."

The cops in the back row did not lower their guns, but at that moment, Officer Lola Sanchez trotted across the stage and placed herself in front of young Laudermaelk. She raised her head and shouted, "Are we here to slaughter children?"

The room was silent again for half a minute before the first rifle barrel dropped from sight. The others quickly followed suit. I walked across the vast stage, unarmed, and took the one assault rifle from AJ's hands and kicked the other away. As soon as I had tossed his guns aside, the boy folded himself into my arms and began crying. "I don't want to die," he chanted over and over, shaking his head wildly side-to-side. Loretta Sanchez came up behind me and together we led AJ Laudermaelk off the stage.

One of the SWAT officers approached the steps with handcuffs. I shook my head. "This child has been through enough," I told him. "He isn't a threat to anyone anymore. Take him to a jail cell if you must, but don't do anything to further traumatize him."

CHAPTER FORTY-TWO

The Rockport Chief of Police was suddenly by my side. "That was mighty damn brave of you, Holman."

"Brave?" I fired back at him. "I was scared shitless the whole time. I just knew what had to be done and I knew the situation I was in. Obviously the kid wasn't a 'suicide by cop' type. He was crying out for help. He didn't want to hurt anyone…"

"But he'd already killed one student…"

"More than one," I told the man. "I've got proof, solid proof in the form of more than one video of the event, that he killed his friend, Johnny Dominguez, at Sea Fair by pushing him out of a gondola on the Ferris wheel. It's a good bet that he killed that classmate of his we found on North Beach in Corpus, and there may well be others we haven't found yet. I'd bet money that the kid isn't mentally stable. But, I think the guilt rests firmly on the father. I think Ames Laudermaelk created this monster."

"Now wait just a cotton-pickin' minute," the chief back-pedaled. "You can't go pointing fingers at people like Ames Laudermaelk. Ames and his family *built* Aransas County. Hell man, they are the county. The Laudermaelk family built much of this part of Texas."

"Then I guess I better be pointing a finger at the entire county, and maybe a few more counties in this part of the state. Ames Laudermaelk is a bully on a bigger scale then his son could ever be. He's a bully in the courtroom and a bully in his politics. What's more, I believe that he's a racist. He bullied you and your department into turning a blind eye when his son pushed his friend off that carnival ride, a young man who Ames himself told me was 'just another dirty Mexican.' And I'll bet it isn't the first time he's twisted the truth with the help of the establishment."

"You have no right," the police chief roared indignantly.

"Sorry, sir," I replied, "but I have every right, and evidence to back up my claims."

The chief went silent for a few moments before changing the subject. "So, how did you know that the Laudermaelk kid wasn't going to blow your brains out? I still think you had some huge *cajones* to face him like that."

"I used to teach a Confrontation course at the Los Angeles Police Academy," I confessed. "I'd had some experience with these situations and did a lot of psychological study of so-called criminal types as well.

"I can't say that a lot of my students took my teachings to heart, especially when you look at situations like the Rodney King fiasco, but the ones who did made a difference. We de-escalated quite a few hostage situations and saved more than one life."

"I still can't believe that Ames Laudermaelk…"

"Believe it." I interrupted him. "I've got plenty of evidence to share when the time is right."

Johnny's So Long at the Fair

When I walked out of Martha Luigi Auditorium the local police officers were busy putting their rifles and vests into the backs of their units. There was an air of euphoria as none of them had been shot or killed and they would all be going home to their families tonight.

Police work has been described as days and weeks of utter boredom followed by a few intense minutes of excitement, danger and fear. I could attest to the truth in this.

I stood by and watched them process young AJ Laudermaelk. I was pleased to see that they didn't put cuffs on the boy. Loretta Sanchez, Danny Lazlo and another officer who I'd worked with in the past, placed AJ in the back of a police SUV and stood beside the car door, chatting with the boy through a slightly cracked window to keep him calm. When they were ready to leave, Danny got in the back of the cop car with AJ.

I got in my Saab and followed them down Live Oak Street to the county lockup. When they placed him in a holding cell, there was a psychological counselor waiting to interview AJ. They had the boy calmed down and ready to talk when Ames Laudermaelk came blustering through the door.

The man cast red devil eyes in my direction. "What the fuck is going on here," he shouted. "Do you know that this is my son you're holding here? Do you know who I am? And do you realize the consequences of what you've done tonight? There will be some heads rolling and a few of you will be looking for work a long way from Texas, if you'll ever work again in law enforcement."

Danny Lazlo stepped forward. "With all due respect, sir," he told the man. "Your son has probably killed at least three people and threatened a few others, including some sworn peace officers. Now if you wish to represent your son in a court of law, you'll have to wait until the county district attorney has built his case. When all the "I's" are dotted and the 'Ts' are crossed, we'll be happy to set you as the attorney of record..."

Ames Laudermaelk looked like he was having a stroke. His face turned a bright vermillion and his eyes appeared to be popping out of his head.

"This is totally unacceptable," he screamed. "You'll be hearing from the governor and from both our US senators. God damn it. I'm Ames Laudermaelk! And this is my son. You have no right to treat us like common criminals."

I cleared my throat softly and when Ames turned to look at me, I said, "Sir, your son has committed acts that are against the law. I suspect that you've probably committed ten times the illegal acts that your son is accused of and I'll happily research that, whether I have a client paying me or not. Right out of the box I can help make a serious case against you for spousal abuse. I was the one who found your wife after you beat her within an inch of her life. Do you want to deny that one?"

"You!" he screamed, "You, you California liberal fuck. You have no business here in Texas. You don't have a clue how things are done down here. When I speak to the governor, we will send you packing, if you don't have an unfortunate accident before you can leave."

Lola Sanchez stepped up between us. "Mr. Laudermaelk? That sounds like a threat against Mr. Holman's life..."

"You bet your sweet female ass it is!" he screamed, in front of half the Rockport Police department. "Now release my son or you'll all be looking for work a long way away from this county."

The Rockport Chief of Police pushed his way through the crowd and stood toe to toe with Ames Laudermaelk, looking him right in the eye. "Ames, I think you've overstepped your authority this time. If you'll turn around to face the wall, I'm going to have to arrest you for threatening to kill one of our Rockport citizens." As the chief held his hands out to Danny Lazlo for a pair of handcuffs, he began reciting his Miranda card from memory. When Ames Laudermaelk started to walk away, two officers grabbed him, one on each side, and forced him against the wall while the chief cuffed his wrists.

Laudermaelk swore like a sailor, threatening to have me killed and any Rockport cop who stood against him as well. When he was given his one required phone call, Laudermaelk demanded to be put through to the governor. He recited a special phone number from memory.

Governor Abbott answered on the third ring and listened to Laudermaelk's rambling for half a minute and then asked to speak to someone in charge.

We all held our breaths. Would the governor stand up for his attorney buddy and demand we turn him loose?

Our answer came quickly. "I'm not sure why this man called me on my *private* line. I've given this number out to very few people, and all of them I've cautioned to call me only in a dire emergency. This man, Laudermaelk, says you are holding him on criminal charges and has also mentioned something about his son.

I was recently briefed on a shooting at Rockport High School which I think involved this man's son. This report already seems to have gone viral in the media.

"I'll leave this to your department to sort out. The state of Texas cannot and will not be involved in any high school shooting event. Please tell your prisoner there not to try and contact my office again."

At this point, the San Patricio County District Attorney came through the door. "Is this Ames Laudermaelk you're holding?" he asked. "If so, I have a few charges of my own to file against this man. There are several cases pending in my Sinton courtroom where folks have had their civil rights violated by this man."

CHAPTER FORTY-THREE

I ended up spending most of that afternoon and evening at police headquarters. I shared the most compelling of my cell phone evidence videos of young AJ pushing Johnny Dominguez to his death from the carnival ride and it was taken into public record. Yolanda helped me establish the chain of evidence as she had kept excellent records of the citizens who had submitted these files to us, with exact times and dates.

All the while, Ames Laudermaelk could be heard shouting from his cell in the next building. One of the county corrections officers came over to the squad room to tell us that the man had almost shouted himself hoarse.

"Laudermaelk says he has information for us that can indict the governor, the lieutenant governor and the secretary of state of serious crimes if we'll turn him loose," the man told us. "Is anyone interested in coming over to the cells to interview him?"

The chief of police snorted out a laugh. "Everyone knows the governor and his people have committed crimes. Tell Laudermaelk we'll be happy to hear his stories in a day or two, but he's staying put until a judge holds a bail hearing on Monday morning. And that's if he's even going to be granted bail. Personally, I think old Ames is a serious flight risk. Rumor has it that he owns a large beach house just a few hours across the border in Ciudad Madero." The district attorneys of two counties, the Aransas county sheriff and a number of peace officers all nodded agreement.

Meanwhile, in one of the interview rooms, Danny Lazlo and a criminal psychologist from the University of Texas, Dr. Werner Stuab, were talking with AJ Laudermaelk. Loretta Sanchez invited me into the small dark space beside the room, where we could observe what was said through a one-way mirror. AJ seemed to be unsure of who he was or why he was here. One minute he would be tearful and contrite for what he had done, the next, he was sitting tall, spouting out hateful racial slurs.

"Dominguez deserved to die." He screeched at one point. "He didn't know his place. My *father* says that all these uppity Mexicans need to be sent back home…

"And Candy had to die as well. My father and his slob friends had soiled her, corrupted her, and made her into a foul slut, just like my father had tried to make my mother into. A strumpet, he always called her when he didn't know I was listening."

And then he gave a loud sob and seemed to collapse into himself. "He treated mom worse than he treated Mexicans," he said in a soft whisper. "But he had no place to send her home to, so he just beat her up and belittled her. Then he stayed at his condo in Austin to avoid her."

"AJ?" Dr. Stuab spoke, placing a hand on the boy's shoulder.

AJ shook the hand off and turned his head to glare at the psychologist. "You don't know, you weren't there," Then with another loud sob, he cried. "No one was there! No one was *ever* there for my mom. Dad made her volunteer for all those bullshit charities. He threatened to cast her aside if she didn't make him look good, then he beat her up anyway, saying she never was good enough to bear the Laudermaelk name."

I noticed the psychologist's eyebrows rising with interest, but he gave no comment.

"When he'd had a few drinks," AJ continued, "Dad used to tell me how much like my mother I was. He'd tell me that I was just barely worthy of being a Laudermaelk. At times like that, he used to undo the pants of his suit and make me prove my love to him on my knees."

Young AJ closed his eyes, his back going stiff at the memory and ending in a painful, horrific scream. "I wish I was dead!" he shouted. "I wish I'd had the guts to blow my own brains out! My own father made me a sick, lowly sinner and then he laughed at me, just like he always laughed at my mother."

As AJ began hyperventilating, the therapist called out for a doctor who was standing by outside the room. They gave AJ a sedative and led him back to his cell.

Dr. Stuab came to the space off the interview room where Lola Sanchez and I were watching. "Do you understand what you've been watching?" he asked.

"A boy who's been dragged through hell and back by a sick, egomaniacal father," I replied. "I've seen such cases before."

The doctor gave me a questioning look. Lola Sanchez explained to him, "Dave Holman came to us from Los Angeles, California. He was a commander there and dealt with many child abuse cases before he retired to Texas."

Dr. Stuab gave me a knowing glance. "It is good that you are here in Rockport, Mr. Holman. This community has for a long time had a shortage of understanding people in the ranks of law enforcement. I just hope these people will listen to you, and of course, to my recommendations. AJ Laudermaelk needs help, not punishment. He's a bright boy, but his self worth has been shredded by those closest to him; recriminations from his father and watching his mother constantly raped and belittled. If it was up to me, I'd recommend years of therapy rather than jail time."

"I totally agree," I told the man. "AJ Laudermaelk could eventually become a good contributor to society with the right counseling. But can we ever sell our viewpoint to a conservative culture who are mainly out for revenge?"

The doctor shook his head as he closed his notebook. Then he stood and held his hand out to me. "Good luck, Mr. Holman. Maybe we'll meet again in this matter."

"I hope we do," I told him sincerely.

CHAPTER FORTY-FOUR

The Austin American-Statesman was the first newspaper to break the story of the arrest of Ames Laudermaelk and his son. By the next day, when the story made the Corpus Christi Caller-Times, public outcry had already found Laudermaelk Senior to be guilty. He had shown himself to be a racist and a bigot as well as a spousal abuser and a misogynist. A University of Texas law professor wrote a column in the Caller-Times about racism in the legal community under the influence of so-called conservative Christian politicians and attorneys. Ames Laudermaelk was convicted by public opinion before he ever had his day in court.

On Tuesday, I met with the Dominguez family. They were pleased that AJ had been caught and even happier that Ames was also in custody. They told me they didn't hold any grudge against young AJ.

"Were grieving for our son," Melba told me, "But we're also praying for the Laudermaelk boy's mortal soul. We've spoken to our priest. He told us that if we should blame anyone, it's the father."

"We're keeping those other families who lost children in our prayers as well," Jesse chimed in. "That Miranda girl and Candace Keene. They were as much victims of Ames Laudermaelk as was our son.

"So do you have a bill for us, Mr. Holman?" he asked. "I might not be able to pay it in full right away, but I will get your money to you. Believe me; you earned it, going up against that child with his rifle, unarmed."

"I learned a lot here myself," I told them. "I'm going to speak with my partner about it. I think she'll agree with me that we don't need to bill you for all the time and mileage I put in. We've all suffered greatly from Nathan, and we've both lost our homes and possessions. I think will come up with a low, kind of token fee for you. The rest of what I might have earned... well, consider it a donation to help you rebuild and get back on your feet."

"Oh, Mr. Holman," Melba began, "We couldn't let you do that."

"It's what I want to do," I told her. "I've got my retirement from Los Angeles and my partner had much of our office insured... Oh, and please call me Dave. Yolanda and I have come to think of you as friends."

By the following Thursday, Laudermaelk's wife, Agnetta, had come forward to tell Rockport Police about the years of abuse she had suffered. She told of horrendous beatings and senseless rapes by the attorney, and of being tied up, gagged and hung from the clothing rail in a bedroom closet while her husband entertained his political friends in the other room.

"My husband always told me I'd only embarrass him with my ignorance if I was permitted to play hostess when he had parties or meetings in our home," she sobbed. "He hired pretty young things who really *were* ignorant as hostesses, calling them his nieces. He told me all I was good for was being a pretty face that could earn him credit with various charities around Rockport."

By the following week, Agnetta Laudermaelk had sold her story to Texas Monthly magazine, driving the final nail in the coffin of Ames Laudermaelk's legal career.

Just after the Texas Monthly article was published, I received a large check in the mail from Agnetta Laudermaelk. The accompanying letter stated that she had heard of my efforts in bringing down her husband and also that I had spoken up for her son, asking leniency for young AJ because of what he'd been through. "Please use some of this to pay for your services to the Dominguez family," she had written. "I have also sent them money to try and make things right for what my son did to their boy. I know money can never be enough to replace a child, but I want to do the best I can for them. God knows that Ames left enough cash stashed around the house as well as money in various local banks.

"I've spoken with AJ at the juvenile facility, and I know he feels bad for what he did. He doesn't understand what possessed him although we both know he was trying to win his father's love and affection, wouldn't you agree Mr. Holman?"

Word on the street was that after his story made the press, Ames Laudermaelk had been blackballed from all his clubs and legal societies. Efforts were underway to disbar him in Texas, as well as two or three other states where he had practiced his trade.

I wondered how all this affected the Texas political machine. Would there still be unmarked cars with special officers to do the bidding of their political masters, like the squads that had stopped me in Austin, or the boys who combed through the wreckage of my office after Hurricane Nathan to steal the evidence I'd collected?

Looking over Yolanda's shoulder at the news on her computer, I noticed that we had some new young candidates willing to go up against the establishment in next year's November elections, men and women who promised that they would only accept funding from individuals; no churches or big corporations.

According to the Texas Monthly article, Agnetta Laudermaelk was using a big chunk of Ames' money to start her own political action committee in support of democratic women running for public office all across the state, and there were quite a few stepping up to file for public offices in local cities and counties, right up to the seats currently held by one of our Republican senators. At Yolanda's urging, I sent some of the money Agnetta had paid me for working the Dominguez case as a donation to her Women in Texas Politics PAC.

I also heard through Loretta Sanchez that Candace Keene's family claimed they had already disowned their 'wild child' so they had no time or reason for grieving. Mrs. Keene had told detectives that they knew of their daughter's drinking and other escapades and did not approve, adding that they had given up on Candace some years ago when she stopped going to church and told them she didn't believe in the Bible or the word of God. They let her live under their roof in hopes she would come around and repent her sins. Obviously, she had not and now God was punishing her. It was all out of their hands.

Miranda Watkins's mother, who lived in a small mobile home, was extremely poor. Hurricane Nathan had caused major damage to her abode, but she had no insurance or savings, so she and Miranda had continued living in the wreckage. When Yolanda and I went to call on her and express our condolences, we found her packing a single old cardboard suitcase.

"We're sorry for your loss," my partner told her, holding out her hand. Ms. Watkins gave us a skeptical look, her eyes traveling down Yolanda and up my frame. My partner extended her arm toward the woman's shoulder in an attempt at a hug. At first, the woman stiffened, but then she started to weep and returned Yolanda's hug. When they separated, she was smiling.

"Thank you," she coughed out. "I don't know who you are, but thank you."

I took a step closer and held out my hand. "My name is Dave Holman. I'm the private detective who investigated the Laudermaelks, both father and son, and saw that they were brought to justice."

The woman's smile faded a bit, then brightened again. She cleared her throat and said, "Call me Madge." She hesitated a moment, then spoke again. "I heard about you. You're the one who walked right up to AJ and took his guns away. I don't know what to think of all this. AJ was always very good to my daughter. While I knew his family had money, he never looked down on us. He was always respectful when he talked to me. Sometimes, he'd bring us takeout food from restaurants and we'd sit and eat together like a family. And then, suddenly, my Miranda went and took her life. Her father deserted me before she was born, but Miranda was a blessing, worth all the troubles of bringing her up for the love we shared. Now I have nothing." Her eyes began to tear up again.

My daughter was all I had in this world. Now I don't have a home or a daughter. The county has told me I have to vacate my trailer. They gave me extra food stamps and enough money to buy a Greyhound bus ticket out of Rockport, so I guess I'll go up to Waco and see if my sister and her husband will take me in."

CHAPTER FORTY-FIVE

By the time all the dust had settled, Rockport had rebuilt many of the structures destroyed by Hurricane Nathan and was getting ready for Sea Fair 2018. We'd had a tough year as Nathan's destruction had severely cut back the city and county tax revenue. The damaged hotels and restaurants had created a negative effect on the summer's tourism and many of our regular "snowbirds" had gone elsewhere. In spite of this, the community rallied and came together behind the slogan "Rockport Strong!"

Yolanda and I had found new digs in a building that had survived pretty well and just needed some repairs to the roof and one wall. On March 5th we were able to move into our new second floor apartment overlooking Little Bay with a store-front office below that used to house a golf cart and kayak rental agency.

Although I still felt a kind of loyalty to Betsy, just east of town at the Bottle Brothel, our new place was about four-hundred paces from the big Spanky's Liquor on State Route 35, and the HEB grocery store just across the highway from Spanky's.

Rusty's hadn't reopened yet, so many of my friends in the Rockport Police would drop by the Holman Agency for a taste. Yolanda had bought a half-dozen fancy Adirondack Chairs in pastel colors which she placed on the balcony of our flat overlooking the water. It was not uncommon to see all those chairs occupied by policemen, with me standing, leaning against the porch railing, like today.

"So, are you planning to have a booth for your elephant rescue this year?" Officer Sanchez asked Yolanda.

"I am," my partner replied, "but this year I've requested a spot facing *away* from the carnival. I don't want Holman distracted by anything that might get him started on another crazy crusade."

Everyone present laughed at that, but the thought sent a small shiver down my spine. I wasn't ready to see another child crushed in the workings of some mechanical joy ride. I wasn't even sure I wanted anything to do with another Sea Fair, but how could I explain this to Yolanda? I'd just have to wait and see how everything went over the next few weeks.

ABOUT THE AUTHOR

Skoot Larson is a native Los Angelino, a musician, music critic and a Viet Nam veteran. He has also worked as a disc jockey, actor, speech therapist, stand-up comedian, behavioral counselor and streetcar conductor. His previous works include the Lars Lindstrom Zen-Jazz Mystery series, a black-humor novel about health care in America entitled "Apollo Issue," and a political humor novel, "The Palestine Solution, and the King Irv fantasy series" Skoot lives with his two cats, Miles and Dexter, in Rockport, Texas.